"Cassandra, I can't understand why you think it's necessary to make this trip to Kentucky to ask your caretaker's blessing before you'll decide to marry me," Tony balked.

"Pop's the nearest thing I have to a family—or father. I guess in some ways I'm traditional—I want Pop to meet you."

Cassie was actually as puzzled as Tony about why she wanted to make this trip—or why she hadn't told Pop that they were coming. Her mind was made up, even though she hadn't given Tony a definite answer. *She was going to marry him.* He had been right—love could come later. After all, she'd thought she loved him once, until David. Maybe what she felt for David was just an illusion. Anyway, she couldn't have made him happy, and now he was back in St. Louis. Dr. McBride was a closed chapter in her life; no need for her to look back. She might as well face it— she was like Tony.

Then, from out of the recesses of her mind, a scene played before her of a picnic by a splendorous waterfall and of David's holding her and saying, "But are you happy, Cassie? Are you happy?"

Dear Reader,

The Cherish Romance™ you are about to read is a special kind of romance written with you in mind. It combines the thrill of newfound romance and the inspiration of a shared faith. By combining the two, we offer you an alternative to promiscuity and superficial relationships. Now you can read a romantic novel—with the romance left intact.

Cherish Romances™ will introduce you to exciting places and to men and women very much involved in today's fast-paced world, yet searching for romance and love with commitment—for someone to cherish and be cherished by. You will enjoy sharing their experiences. Most of all you will be uplifted by a romance that involves much more than physical attraction.

Welcome to the world of Cherish Romance™—a special kind of place with a special kind of love.

Etta Wilson

Etta Wilson, Editor

The Challenged Heart

Anna Lloyd Staton

Cherish
Romances

Thomas Nelson Publishers • Nashville • Camden • New York

To Our Mother
Anne Staton
Whose love and encouragement
have been constant
throughout this endeavor

Published in Nashville, Tennessee, by Thomas Nelson, Inc. and distributed in Canada by Lawson Falle, Ltd., Cambridge, Ontario.

Printed in the United States of America.

All of the characters and events in this book are fictitious. Any resemblance to actual persons, living or dead, or to actual events is purely coincidental.

ISBN 0-8407-7361-7

Chapter One

An early morning mist was rising from the pasture lake as Cassie quietly let herself out of the old Victorian farmhouse.

Carrying a steaming mug of coffee across the wide veranda, she heard a soft whinny from the ridge on the far side of the lake. Even through the mist, she saw the tossing elegant head of her Arabian mare, Nadia, and noted her graceful form as she pranced along the edge of the crimson forest, silhouetted against the autumn hues subdued in the early light.

Cassie took a deep breath and reveled in the tranquility of the crisp morning. Just then, the sun broke through the mist and scattered its radiance on the dewdrops still clinging to the pasture grass. A slight fragrance of wood smoke hung in the air. Somewhere in the distance, a tardy rooster crowed, as the sounds of awakening nature became symphonic.

The slender, young woman with her short cap of dark, lustrous curls yawned and took another sip of coffee. *Cassie, this lethargy will never do,* she told herself. *You have a busy day before you.*

After placing her mug on the porch railing, she strolled across the yard to the board fence and climbed over into the paddock.

As she approached the barn, she heard a snort and recognized the unmistakable sound of Shebazzi, her stallion, demanding his morning meal. "Just be patient,

5

fellow. I'm coming," she called lovingly. She opened the stall door and marveled at the beauty of the proud horse's sinewy structure and his rich mahogany color.

Caressing Shebazzi's muscular neck, Cassie smiled faintly as she saw her reflection in an old mirror that hung on a nearby post. She walked over to the mirror, cracked from age, and lightly ran her finger over the dusty oak frame that encased it. Fond memories ran through her mind like dust particles floating in a shaft of light. The looking glass had been hanging in the same spot for over fifty years—put there by her grandfather, Adam Delaney. She smiled as she thought of the old patriarch, tall and strong like a great oak tree. Her memory of him was vivid—his dry wit, his easy laugh, and his deep, abiding love for his family—and for these Kentucky hills to which she now had returned.

Again she caught her reflection in the cracked mirror and, with a critical eye, she evaluated her well-scrubbed face, checked shirt, and faded jeans. Cassie's dark brown eyes stared intensely at her likeness. Slowly, her slim fingers reached out and gently touched the face on the silvery surface of the old mirror, as if she were trying to reassure herself that it was indeed her image.

"Well, I guess you *are* Cassandra Delaney," she said aloud, as if finally reaching an important decision. "But it certainly is hard to believe that you could be the editor of an important magazine like *Woman's Life*." With a humorless chuckle, she asked herself, "What has happened to you, Cassie? What has happened to you?"

Leaving her question unanswered, she added, "And what about my friends? Would they recognize this Cassandra—with no make-up, no *long* hair, and freckles on her nose?" A faint smile crossed her face as she thought of New York and her life there. It was an exciting life. The pace was fast, the job was challenging, and her friends and business associates were the influential, the famous, and the glamorous.

"Oh, Cassandra," she thought. "It's not whether they

6

would *recognize* you—it's what they would *think* of you." The faint smile left her face as embers of the past stirred bittersweet memories. Still gazing into the mirror, she whispered almost inaudibly, "And, Tony, what would you think? Would you even care? Do you....?"

As the specter of past hurts and disillusionments threatened to engulf her, Cassie walked out of the stall and busied herself with the tasks at hand.

She unlocked the old lean-to that served as a storage room and noticed the door had been repaired. She knew Pop Bailey, the wiry old caretaker, had fixed it. She sighed with thankfulness, realizing once again how much she depended on him. His wisdom and strength were a big part of the reason she had returned to these back hills of Kentucky to begin rebuilding her shattered life.

Old Pop (his real name was Aubry) seemed as much a part of this place as the Victorian farmhouse and the rolling hills. Orphaned in his early teens, he had left his meager Appalachian mountain home, taking nothing with him but a willing back and a cheerful heart, and come to the valley below. There Aubry had met Cassie's grandparents. Young and newly married, they had a dream in their hearts of cleared acres, grazing herds, and growing crops. Aubry had offered his help—and, whether it was the God he believed in or just a mountain boy's luck, he had been here ever since.

As Cassie took the lock from the feed-room door, she heard a moan behind her! Dropping the lock and keys, she ran back into the barn. For a moment, she couldn't see, but, as her eyes adjusted to the darkness inside, she noticed a movement near the ladder to the loft.

"Pop!" she cried as she recognized the crumpled body of her friend!

"Uhh." The moaning was very low and weak.

Cassie looked up and saw a jagged, gaping hole in the floor of the loft above Aubry, and knew that one of the much-needed repairs had been delayed too long.

"Pop, where are you hurt?" she asked with a calmness that belied her pounding heart.

"My back," he whispered, "and I can't move my leg. Go get Doc Dave."

Cassie had heard of the good samaritan who devoted his life to caring for the mountain folk. She hesitated for a moment as her mind questioned the competency of a doctor who practiced so far from modern medical centers with their up-to-date procedures.

"Hurry, Cassie," Pop whispered urgently.

Realizing old Doc Dave would have to do, she dashed from the barn and toward the porch. Vaulting up the steps two at a time, she practically slid across the porch floor and into the back door. Jerking it open, she was inside the kitchen and fumbling for the telephone book. *Dear God, please let the doctor be in*, she prayed.

Cassie was startled to realize that she was praying. It had been a long time. She hoped God wouldn't hold that against her. After all, it was Pop Bailey who counted, and she knew prayer was no stranger to him.

Flipping through the telephone book, Cassie panicked. "What is his last name?" She had heard him called only Doc Dave.

She picked up the receiver and dialed the operator.

"This is Cassandra Delaney at Delaney Farms on Maple Ridge Road. The caretaker has been seriously injured, and I need an ambulance."

"I'm sorry, ma'am, the nearest ambulance service is twenty miles away from where you are, but I'll put you through to Dr. David McBride. Perhaps he can help you."

The operator's voice calmed Cassie. She was amazed at the woman's familiarity with her location. Rural areas were so different from the impersonal, urban surroundings of New York. She never had considered how isolated she was in case of an emergency. Twenty miles from town and two miles off the main road hadn't bothered her until now, but Pop had always been there to depend on.

"Yes, thank you, operator, that'll be fine. Did you say his name is McBride? Is he far from my place?"

"As a matter of fact, Miss Delaney, he lives right down the road from the Old Delaney Place, er, I mean, Delaney Farms," the woman sputtered, embarrassed at the slip of her tongue.

"If you'll get the doctor, please; it's urgent," Cassie cut in abruptly.

The connection was made quickly and, after three short rings, a deep voice answered. "Hello, McBride speaking."

"Dr. McBride, this is an emergency!" Cassie's demand sounded curt as her panic once again mounted.

"Who is this?" The pleasant voice took on an even deeper timbre that was all business.

"This is Cassie Delaney. Pop Bailey has had a bad fall in the barn and I'm afraid to move him."

"I'll be right there," he interrupted. The phone clicked, ending the terse conversation.

"But wait! You don't know where I live! Don't you want directions to my place?" Cassie asked the silent receiver.

She quickly dialed again, but there was no answer.

"I can't believe it—I can't believe it," she cried aloud in frustration. "God, please let him know where I live."

Her large, dark eyes filled with tears as she rushed down the long hall in search of a blanket.

She jerked two blankets from the linen closet's store of fresh, soft linens, and ran toward the back door.

Slamming the door behind her, she bolted down the steps. Cassie winced as she turned her ankle at the bottom step, but the pain didn't slow her pace. Her thoughts were only for Pop.

"Pop, here I am. Just hang on." Her voice quavered, even though she tried to appear calm for him. As her slender arms reached out to cover him, she hoped her panic would not be evident to him.

What should I do now? Cassie mentally asked herself, as she tried to recall her first aid class of ten years before.

"I'm afraid to move you with your leg folded under you," she said to the injured man. Hearing her own voice seemed to give her courage. She added silently, *I've got to do something until the doctor comes—that is, if he comes.* An overwhelming sense of helplessness possessed Cassie. *Oh God, please help me—please help me,* she pleaded silently.

Outside the barn, she heard the crunch of gravel, as a vehicle made its way up the drive. Cassie looked at her watch. It had been only a few minutes since she had called. By some miracle, could it be the doctor?

Through the open barn door she saw a landrover jerk to a halt. A tall man in his middle thirties got out of the rover and strode purposefully toward the barn.

"Thank you, God. Maybe this man can help," Cassie murmured while she frantically turned her attention back to the injured man as he moaned once again.

Leaning over Pop, she heard his shaky voice calling, "Doc Dave."

"I'm right here, Pop," said a vaguely familiar deep voice.

Cassie gasped and looked up. The newly arrived stranger was towering directly over her. "Sorry I startled you," he said as he offered his hand in greeting. "I'm David McBride. I own the farm next to you."

Cassie hesitated for a split second before taking his hand. "You're Dr. McBride?" she questioned skeptically. She found it hard to believe that this ruggedly handsome man could be the "samaritan" Pop spoke of so often.

"Yes, I'm Dr. McBride," he said, as his strong, competent hand firmly shook hers.

Once again, Pop called for Doc Dave, only this time his voice sounded stronger. Cassie quickly moved aside, and the doctor knelt to give his full attention to the old man lying awkwardly on the barn floor.

"Doc," Pop said weakly, "I'm glad you're here."

While David slowly examined Pop, the old man became more lucid. "How'd ya get here so quick?" he asked the doctor.

Examing Pop's head, David replied, "I'll tell you later. Besides this goose egg on your head, where else does it hurt?"

"My leg is hurtin' awful!"

The doctor gently took the older man's right foot. He slowly moved it forward as he intently observed his patient. Pop winced with pain, but didn't make a sound. When the leg was straightened out in front of him, Dr. McBride pushed up the pants leg and began a careful examination of the injured limb. His long, well-shaped fingers stopped just below the knee, and he murmured something under his breath.

"What's that ya say, Doc?" inquired Aubry.

"I said you're a lucky man—I don't believe your leg is even broken. What about your back?"

"It's still hurtin' some, but my head is pounding like a steam locomotive!"

"What did you expect after bouncing around on it? I've told you a hundred times to stay on the ground! Aubry, you know a man of your age shouldn't be climbing up in the barn loft. You have a badly sprained ankle and a bruised leg and maybe a slight concussion. I want you to go to bed and stay out of the loft! As I said, you're a lucky man," the doctor delcared.

"I don't believe in luck. It's the good Lord what looks after me, and He can look after me as well in the loft as on the ground," the old man retorted, regaining some of his strength as the pain subsided.

"Then why did you fall?"

"Well," the old man drawled, "have you ever heard of Divine Appointments?" With a twinkle in his steel gray eyes, Aubry looked at Cassie. "This here is my Cassie I

11

told you about, and Cassie, this here is Doc Dave."

The doctor looked puzzled for a moment and then turned to look into the deep brown eyes of an equally puzzled Cassie.

David addressed Cassie in a firm tone. "If you'll get his bed ready, I'll help him to the cabin."

"Certainly, Doctor," she replied in a subdued voice, as she turned toward the door. Outside in the bright morning sunlight, she realized she felt drained of all energy—and remembered that neither she nor the horses had had a morning meal.

The old log cabin stood some hundred yards behind the main house and was nestled in a forest blazing with red and gold-leafed maple trees. Letting herself in, she marveled at the sense of peace in the four-room cabin. The feeling always had been the same; she had experienced it even as a child when she had come here. Pop would spin exciting tales about his life and then tell her about the God he believed in.

After pulling the covers back, Cassie went across the room to open the door for the two men. The strong, young doctor was practically carrying the aging man across the porch. David seemed oblivious to the burden as he listened intently to something Pop was saying.

"Well, Pop, you surely gave me a scare. Why didn't you tell me you weren't supposed to be climbing around in the barn?" Cassie asked as the men entered. Before Pop could answer, she continued, "You've insisted on taking care of me these past few weeks; now I get my turn. It's to bed with you, and I'll run up to the house and warm the vegetable soup, along with the fresh bread that I made yesterday. Would you like some, Doctor?"

"Yes, I would. I'll go up to the house as soon as I finish examining this stubborn friend of ours," the doctor said with a warm smile.

Back inside her own house, Cassie took the large tureen of soup out of the refrigerator. She poured a generous portion into a saucepan and placed it on the gas stove to heat. The aromas of homemade soup, fresh bread, and perking coffee soon filled the country kitchen.

Cassie had almost finished her preparations when, through the bay window, she saw the easy gait of Dr. David McBride as he approached the house. Hidden from his view, Cassie observed him carefully. Ruggedly handsome, he was well over six feet tall with thick, sun-streaked hair. A plaid wool shirt and faded jeans emphasized his lean, muscular physique. He evidenced self-confidence and strength in every step, and his firm, square jaw seemed to denote a man of purpose.

Cassie was surprised to note her heart had begun to pound as he approached the door.

Realizing her palms were clammy, she was alarmed. *What is wrong with me? I'm accustomed to good-looking men! I hardly know this man; he's just a country doctor.*

Pushing the disturbing thoughts from her mind, she quickly dried her hands and went to the door. She greeted him with deliberate composure. "Come in, Dr. McBride. Pop's lunch is just about ready." With a confidence she did not feel she added, "And so is yours."

"Thank you, Miss Delaney. The smell of that bread and soup is really tempting but I won't have time for more than a cup of coffee, after all. I left some unfinished business at home, and I have to see some patients this afternoon. You know some of my house calls are forty miles away," he explained with a disarming smile as he walked into the warmth of the cheerful kitchen.

Cassie, even more aware of his rugged good looks, felt suddenly small and helpless in her own kitchen as she looked up into the kind blue eyes of this giant who seemed to fill the room.

A feeling stirred inside her that she did not like. Somehow she wasn't the self-reliant Cassandra Delaney of *Woman's Life* fame. She seemed to need a strength outside her own, one to surround her and protect her from hurt and disillusionment. *She sensed in this man that strength.* Almost giving in to the impulse to lean toward him, she shook her head as if to clear it and stepped back instead.

If the doctor noticed, he gave no indication as Cassie regained her composure and said, "Have a seat, Doctor." Cassie pointed to the ladder-back chair beside the round oak table. Late-blooming mums with large bronze and yellow blossoms filled a brass pitcher in the center. Bright yellow placemats complimented the flowers and brought a cheery elegance to the setting.

"How do you like your coffee, Dr. McBride?" she inquired.

"Black, please," he said as he sat and stretched his long legs across the breakfast room in a moment of relaxation.

Cassie turned from him and poured two cups of coffee into the same china cups that her grandmother had used. The cream-colored china with the border of platinum and delicate flowers had been treasured carefully down through the years.

She handed a cup and saucer to McBride and noticed how strange the delicate cup looked in his hands. Yet, for all their size, his hands had been skilled and efficient when examining Aubry.

He sat up straight as he took the coffee from Cassie and she could feel the warmth of his appraising gaze. She turned to get her cup and the loaf of bread on the counter. He did not see the startled look on her face when he asked, "Tell me, Miss Delaney, what brings you back to Delaney Farms?"

Cassie sliced the bread before she turned to answer. She needed time to think.

Knowing she could not give the *real* reason for her hasty return, she groped for an answer that would satisfy him. Balancing a basket of bread in one hand and

14

her coffee in the other, she walked over to the table and casually sat down.

"Delaney Farms is my home," she began. "I lived here briefly with my grandparents after the death of my parents, and I still regard this as home even though they've both been dead for several years. I always come back when I can find a break in my busy schedule," she quietly answered.

His penetrating blue eyes scanned her face, as if expecting her to continue. Cassie felt a blush rising to her cheeks. For a moment, she felt as if he had looked into the depths of her heart and had seen the frustration and emptiness hidden there.

Under his intense gaze, she knew her composure would soon crumble. This man seemed to pierce right through the facade. She dropped her eyes, afraid that he would discern the truth.

Finally he spoke, "Cassandra—may I call you Cassandra?" She nodded as he continued to speak. "I understand you're a successful career woman. Pop is mighty proud of all your accomplishments. He told me that you're the editor of *Woman's Life* magazine. It must have taken a great deal of commitment and effort to attain that position at the age of twenty-eight. How's your book coming along?" He chuckled at her surprised look. "Yes, he's told me about that, too. A mystery, isn't it?"

Cassie smiled, somewhat chagrined that David knew so much about her. "Pop really did fill you in about me! Do you know what I had for breakfast this morning?" she laughingly asked as she tried to divert the conversation to safer channels.

"Well, from my observation, professionally speaking of course, I'd say you forgot to eat," he lightly retorted.

"Right you are, Doctor. That was an astute diagnosis, sir," she continued the bantering. "Do you recommend any special treatment?"

"As a matter of fact, I do. Cut down on your coffee

and eat a well-balanced meal three times a day. From the looks of you, I'd say you've skipped several. These mountain folks would say you're looking right 'peaked.' "

"Is that how *you'd* describe me, Doctor?" Cassie's vanity couldn't resist the challenge.

He paused for a moment as his eyes appraised her appreciatively. Then, with a crooked grin lending an air of mischief to his face, he drawled, "Not exactly. I'd say you look rather frail and in need of a little peace of mind." Noting the startled look on Cassie's face, he continued, "There's a furrow on that beautiful brow and a storm lurking in those flashing eyes."

Slowly, David stood up and, reaching down, he took her chin in his hand and lifted her face so that her gaze would meet his! The crooked smile was gone as he said, with a new tone of intensity, "And you are indescribably lovely."

Cassie sat in stunned silence as David abruptly turned and left the kitchen. A moment later she heard his truck drive away—and a deep sense of loneliness engulfed her.

Chapter Two

Mid-morning light filtered through leaded glass windows and cascaded onto the lace coverlet overspreading Cassie's tall poster bed. The rich patina of heartpine floors and mahogany furnishings in the large bedroom reflected a warm glow in the stream of light.

Cassie sat up in bed, startled. She looked at the clock over the mantle of the small, brick fireplace in the corner of the room and realized that it had stopped. *No wonder I overslept*, she thought, noticing that the clock had stopped its hourly chimes at midnight.

Reluctantly, she pulled back the covers and stepped onto the soft wool rug beside her bed. The rug, worn but still beautiful, had been one of the last gifts her grandfather had given her grandmother before his death. It had been imported from China.

This room had been their room; this bed, their bed. It had known the abiding joy of their most intimate moments for fifty years—the joy of a passionate love shared for a lifetime. That was what she had wanted for Tony and herself, she thought bitterly.

The warm feeling of pleasure Cassie usually felt in this room was strangely absent this morning. She felt vaguely uneasy. Then she remembered the events of the day before and the source of her anxiety.

Pop, she thought. *I need to get his breakfast. I bet he's grumbling about not having his coffee yet*.

Her tempo increased as she retrieved a pair of designer jeans and a crimson pullover from her closet. Noting her wanness, she decided to give her lips a touch of color and to run a brush through her tousled curls. She donned a pair of soft leather boots, a gift from Tony. She surveyed her image in the full-length mirror.

"Well, that looks more like you, Cassandra. Would you be expecting a visitor?" she asked aloud. With that she hurried down the stairs.

In a short time, Cassie had a tray ready to take to Pop. She made sure that it was a well-balanced meal—fresh-squeezed orange juice, an omelet, and toasted English muffins, along with a fresh pot of coffee. Remembering Dr. McBride's comments about her own diet, she carried enough for two on the tray.

"I surely don't want to look 'peaked,' " she drawled as she glanced at her slender reflection in the old hall-tree mirror that stood by the kitchen door.

"I wonder what he meant by 'peaked?' In New York, I'd be perfect—well, in Rome, do as the Romans do, or 'follow the doctor's orders,' " she mused.

Cassie was carefully maneuvering down the steps with the heavily laden tray when the familiar truck of David McBride drove up the winding lane. Pulling to a stop in front of her, he opened the door and stepped out.

"Looks like you could use some help," David greeted her as he took the tray.

"Well, Dr. McBride, you rescue me again," Cassie said lightly as she tried to push aside yesterday's disturbing memories.

"My pleasure, milady," he assured her, with a mischievous grin.

"Did you finish your house calls?" Cassie inquired.

"Well, as a matter of fact, I did, but they were a little more complicated than I expected. I didn't get home until around three this morning," the doctor explained.

"Oh? Nothing too serious, I hope."

"Well, it could have been, but I'm thankful that everything turned out fine. A fifteen-year-old girl gave birth to twins last night, and for a while it looked as if we were going to lose the mother and the babies," he responded.

"How tragic. Fifteen years old, you say? Unwed mother?"

"No. The girls here marry young and have large families," he explained.

"What was wrong? Couldn't she make it to the hospital? Did you happen by or did they call?" Her journalist's interest was aroused.

He looked at her quizzically. "You don't know much about the people here, do you? I thought you grew up here!"

"I came here during the summers, and I lived here briefly after my parents died. Then I went back East to school, and I haven't been back much since then," she answered coolly.

"I see," he said, pausing for a moment before he continued. "These women don't go to the hospital to have their children, Cassie."

"Why?" was her quick response.

'Because they can't afford to and because they've always had their babies at home. Until I came, they were dependent on midwives. The midwives have done well in normal births, but, for complicated ones, the mortality rate is extremely high. Now we're beginning to see an impressive reduction in the number of infant deaths," he finished, with a note of pleased excitement creeping into his voice.

"Why did you choose this place to set up your practice? Is your home near here?" She realized the expression on his face ignited a spark of interest in her that went beyond her normal journalist's curiosity.

"No, my family is in St. Louis, or at least my father is. My mother is dead. After my residency, I did some special studies on black lung disease and, as I traveled from coal mine to coal mine in the hills of West Virginia and Kentucky, I began to really like this section of the country," David explained.

"It must be more than that. These hills are beautiful, but there's no way you can be making the money here that you could in a city."

"You're right. The air's pure, but the pay is slight," he laughed.

"Well, why are you here?" she persisted.

"I've been asked that question before," he hesitated, "most often by my Dad. I'm his only child and this is not his idea of a successful career. I guess the only way I can explain it is to say it's my 'calling.'"

"Your what?" she asked, mystified.

"I feel that helping the mountain folk is what God wants me to do with my life," he explained quietly.

"Do you really think God cares what you do with your life?" she asked with an uneasy look in her dark eyes.

"I know He does," David said with quiet conviction.

The conversation ended abruptly when they reached Pop's doorstep. As the couple entered the front door, they found Pop out of bed and fully dressed. The wiry old man looked comical as he sat in front of his small television set staring intently at a cartoon program while he munched a candy bar and drank a glass of chocolate milk!

"Pop," Cassie wailed, "what are you doing out of bed and eating candy for breakfast?"

"Shhh! Just a minute, girl," he replied.

Then, as the program ended, he turned to her and explained, "I'm up because I never miss this program, and I'm eating candy because that's what I always have for breakfast," he retorted.

"What about your back?" she questioned.

"Shore it's stiff and my leg's sore, but I'll jist work it out by moving around," he explained.

The doctor had placed the breakfast tray on the dining table and could barely contain his mirth.

"Well, Aubry, I guess you don't need the doctor's medicine or advice, eh? I told you to stay in bed. How's your head?"

"It's all right this morning. What ya got on that tray?" the old man inquired.

"Your breakfast!" Cassie responded.

"I told ya I had my breakfast. You eat it. Anyway, ain't it a mite late for breakfast?"

"You're right there, Pop. I guess your nurse must have overslept," David said with a twinkle in his eye.

"Dr. McBride, there's plenty for two. Will you join me?" Cassie stammered.

"I would be delighted," the doctor replied.

"How about some coffee, Pop?" Cassie offered.

"Now that would be just fine, I think!" Pop said as the three of them sat down at the small square oak table that had served Aubry's needs for fifty years.

Cassie and David ate heartily, with a minimum of conversation. After the meal, David and Pop went out on the porch. Cassie could hear snatches of their conversation as she cleared away the dishes.

"But you can't leave us, Doc," the old man was saying.

"I know, Aubry. I truly feel that this is where I'm supposed to be, but my father just won't accept that. He still insists I take over his clinic. I was writing him a letter when Cassie called yesterday. I told him 'no' again, but I'm sure that won't be the last of it."

Pop looked at David with sympathetic eyes as he replied, "David, yore Dad loves ya and with a little patience, he'll come 'round one of these days. Jist wait and see."

"Maybe so, but it's hard to forget that look of cold fury on his face when I told him I couldn't marry Priscilla or work for him." David sighed deeply and then added quietly as if to himself, "That's the last time I've seen him."

"People change, Doc," Pop gently reminded.

David paused and then chuckled before answering, "That's true. Who would have believed five years ago that I'd be content living and working here?—And Big Bertha, my rover, is a far cry from the Porsche I had in St. Louis."

"Well, for my money, that rover makes a lot more sense than one of them fancy little bugs zipping all around. Besides Big Bertha's got class, *real* class!"

"You're probably right, Pop, you're probably right. Well, as much as I hate to, I've got to be going. I need to check on Jenny—she had twins early this morning! And from the looks of you, I know you're going to be fine."

"Jenny had twins!" Pop exclaimed brightly just as Cassie walked onto the porch.

"Yes, two fine boys." David responded, then turning to Cassie, "Before I leave, I wanted to issue an invitation—"

"An invitation? What kind?"

"I'll get back around 4:30 day after tomorrow and I'd like to introduce you to some of your neighbors. Earlier you mentioned that you really aren't familiar with the people of the mountains or what their lives are like. I'd like to remedy that situation. Besides, I have someone special for you to meet. You'll really enjoy visiting with him."

Cassie met David's steady gaze and hesitated before answering, "Go with you to see one of your patients, hmmm? I'll have to admit you've piqued my curiosity."

David chuckled at her bewilderment and said, "You'll know two days hence and not 'afore time."

"Do you know how frustrating it is for a journalist not to have all the facts? We hate to be kept in suspense—about anything!"

David smiled warmly and stepped over the porch railing. Turning with a wave of his hand, he added softly, "Milady, I'll pick you up day after tomorrow at 4:30."

Cassie stood with Pop as they watched him walk toward the rover. With one smooth motion he climbed in and waved a final farewell.

The couple stood silently until the truck was out of sight. Then Cassie turned to Pop and asked, "Pop, what's with this doctor? Couldn't he make it in the city?"

"What do ya mean 'make it,' girl?"

"You know. Wasn't he good enough to have a successful practice in the city?"

"Good enough! He graduated at the top of his class and he got his trainin' at one of them big hospitals in the East. He turned down a partnership with them famous doctors, Michael and Farragut, so he could study this here black lung disease. Have ya heard of those doctors?" Pop asked.

"Yes, I know of them. I don't understand why he's here," she persisted.

"Why don't ya ask him?"

"I did. He gave me some story about God 'calling' him here."

The old man turned to look at the girl, and, with a troubled expression, asked, "Don't ya believe God has purposes for people's lives, Cassie? That He calls them to where they can do the most good?"

"I think that it's our right to do what we think is best for us and I can hardly see that starving in these hills is better than living comfortably in New York. It seems to me that, if he received that kind of offer, he ought to go where the money is."

Pop's concern deepened as he looked Cassie straight in the eyes and said, "Cassie, girl, when did ya git so hard? Where'd ya ever git the notion that money is the most important thing in the world?"

Cassie's warm brown eyes turned stormy; she narrowed them slightly and bit at her lower lip. Her voice took on a cold edge as she replied, "About halfway through my sophomore year in college, after my parents died. Then Gramps and Grandmother died, and I

23

found myself totally alone and with very little money. At most places it's OK to have to work your way through school, but, at that school, it was a social stigma to have to work."

"How do ya mean, honey?" Pop inquired gently.

"If you didn't have enough money or didn't wear the right clothes, then you weren't asked to join a sorority. That I could handle, but they wouldn't let me work on the school paper either, and I wanted that in the worst kind of way," she replied bitterly.

"Why did ya stay there?" the old man continued questioning Cassie.

"Because their journalism program is one of the best in the East, and I wanted a degree from there. I knew it would open doors for me, and it did. One thing I learned, money is the key to survival. I vowed that, when I got a job, I'd never be without it again." The girl's beautiful eyes closed for a moment as if trying to blot out the painful memories.

"Oh, Cassie, I wish I could ease yur hurt!" The old man's eyes were misty as he looked at the girl who, for a moment, seemed a stranger to him.

Forcing herself to smile brightly, Cassie said, "Don't worry about me, Pop. That's past history and a lesson well-learned. Now, I've got my feet planted on the success ladder and my head on straight."

Aubry Bailey paused for a second and then responded, "Maybe so, Cassie, maybe so. But I kinda believe the little girl that used to crawl up in my lap and ask me to tell her about how God loved her and what He wanted her to be is still inside ya—"

Cassie turned quickly from Pop before he could see the tears gathering in her large dark eyes.

How could she tell him…she was afraid *that* Cassie was gone forever.

Chapter Three

Cassie wasted the two days she had set aside to work on her novel. The quiet house offered no interruptions, but a restlessness and uneasiness stirred her heart, distracting her more than a thousand phone calls. Her manuscript lay untouched.

She struggled with painful memories: sometimes a longing for Tony that would end in anger; at other times frustration and disgust with her own procrastination; and then pellmell her mind would turn to Dr. David McBride. The handsome physician kept invading her thoughts.

Finally, in mid-afternoon of the second fruitless day, Cassie walked away from her empty typewriter in exasperation. Relieved, she heard Pop's familiar rap at the back door.

"Well, finished your book yet?" Pop asked when she opened the door.

"Pop," Cassie laughed, "you don't write a book in two days! It takes a long time."

"Does it now? Then, I shore hope it takes at least five years. It does this old heart good to wake up in the morning, just knowing yur up here in yore grandparents' old place...Yep, does my heart good," he said as he walked into the kitchen with an armload of firewood. "Figured I'd better get ya some wood in here. My bones are tellin' me real cold weather is a comin' soon."

Cassie smiled at this dear old man whom she loved so much. "Pop, are you still telling the weather by your bones? Don't you ever just listen to the weather report?"

"Now girl, I've lived a long time and there's two things I've learnt I can depend on—my bones for the weather and the good Lord for everything else." Without stopping to take a breath, Pop asked, "You still going with Doc Dave this afternoon?"

"Well of course I am. I'm looking forward to meeting one of his patients."

"Is that the *only* reason yur going?" Pop baited her.

Cassie raised one eyebrow as she looked at Pop and lightly countered, "Pop Bailey, what are you fishing for?"

"Shucks, I ain't never been no good at tryin' to git information by asking sneaky questions! I was just hopin' that maybe ya might be lookin' forward a bit to bein' with the doctor. Ya know, as men go, he ain't half bad lookin'. He's a real good man and," Pop added with emphasis, "he ain't spoken for."

Cassie burst into laughter at the wistful expression on the old man's face.

"First you fall out of the loft and mumble something about 'Divine Appointments' and now you're talking like this. If I didn't know better I'd think you were trying to match me up with David McBride!" Cassie teased.

Pop didn't answer but stooped down and started to stack the firewood in the wood box next to the back door. "Maybe it ain't me that's a doin' the matching," was all he would say.

"What is this 'Divine Appointment' anyway?"

"Ain't too difficult to explain," Pop said matter-of-factly. "Jist the good Lord decides two people orta meet and then He goes 'bout 'ranging it."

"Pop," Cassie said lamely, "David is a fine man, I can see that...but he's just not my type. Do you understand what I'm saying?" she finished as she stooped down and gently kissed Aubry's weathered cheek.

Pop looked at her and tenderly said, "Ah, girl, I heard yur words and I understand exactly what ya be saying." Standing up, he placed an arm around her shoulders. "Now ya best be a gettin' ready, 'cause Doc's goin' to be here before ya know it."

Cassie grinned while knowing in her heart that this dear, stubborn soul had not believed a word she had said.

It was a little after 4:30 when Cassie heard the land-rover pull into the yard. She grabbed the rust sweater that matched her slacks and met David at the door.

"Looks like you're eager to get started on our visit," David said teasingly as they walked toward Big Bertha.

"I guess you could say I am, after you aroused my curiosity and then refused to satisfy it. Journalists don't like to be left hanging," she bantered back.

"Your curiosity will be put to rest soon enough," he said, "but first I'd like to take a look at those fine horses I've heard so much about."

Puzzled, Cassie turned toward him. "You haven't seen them yet? I thought you were a regular visitor around here."

"Usually it's after dark, and, if you recall, I was too busy on my recent visit to your barn," he added.

"Come on in the barn. I'm always eager to show our beauties off." Cassie led the way as they entered the dark hallway and stopped at Nadia's stall. "Nadia, greet your neighbor," Cassie said, and the chestnut mare answered with a low whinny.

The physician let out a low whistle. "You weren't kidding when you said 'beauty.' I've never seen a better proportioned mare." David walked into the stall and ran his hand down the sleek neck. "Her disposition matches her looks. Seems gentle."

"Thank you. Arabians are people horses. They like affection. She's gentle in the stall but she's plenty spirited

27

under saddle. Shebazzi, our stallion, is equally as fine in looks and temperament. He's out in the pasture, so maybe we can get a glimpse of him when we leave."

The couple walked through the barn and out into the sunlight, just as they heard a whinny from the far side of the lake.

"Oh, there he is now," Cassie pointed. As if right on cue, the proud stallion arched his neck, picked his tail up high, and pranced down the ridge into the woods.

"Those Arabs really know how to put on a show," David chuckled as he paused for a moment to watch the horse thunder out of sight.

"That's one of the qualities I like so much about them. They have real style, but Shebazzi is just a big ham if he thinks he has an audience!" Cassie said as they climbed into the landrover.

Soon they were on the main road going the opposite direction from town, and Cassie relaxed to enjoy the scenery along the winding road. Abruptly David turned from the smooth, paved road onto a dirt one, and they began a bouncing ascent. The road became little more than a two-rut trail. Cassie, acutely aware of the steep dropoff just outside her window, clutched the seat tightly.

"You don't come up here at night, do you?" she inquired, alarmed.

"I do if I'm needed. I'll have to admit it's not the most pleasant ride when it rains or when it's dark. But Big Bertha here is nearly as good as a mountain goat. Relax, I haven't had a wreck yet! Do you see that house there?" David pointed to a tar-papered shack perched on the side of a steep slope about a hundred yards from the road.

"Those people lost two children to typhoid fever four years ago," he continued. "In fact, twenty children died with it when several springs became contaminated. None of them had been immunized. It's just too far to the clinic in town for them to take their kids in for proper health care." David's face grew wistful as he continued, "I've bought an old schoolhouse about four miles from here that someday I'd like to set up as a clinic, but we'd need to staff it with at least two other doctors and several nurses. I just can't afford it, and not many other doctors want this kind of life. But I know one day the right doors will open and it will become a reality."

"How would you support a clinic?" Cassie asked, genuinely interested.

"That's the problem. Unless we could get a government grant or an endowment from an individual, the clinic could not be self-supporting, so I'm just trusting that somehow it'll work out. Meanwhile, I'm doing what I can." A somber look crossed David's face and Cassie realized the doctor was trying to hide his frustration.

"Suppose I did an article on what you're trying to do here. Do you think that might stir some interest in your work?" Cassie asked, sensing the germ of a dramatic human interest story.

"Uhm, that might help, but I didn't know *Woman's Life* carried stories like that," David answered, surprised.

"Occasionally we do if the story is outstanding, but I have other contacts, David, even if *Woman's Life* isn't interested."

"What do you mean not interested? I thought you were the editor. Don't you have final say?" David questioned pointedly.

"Uh—yes and no," Cassie said softly.

David turned off the road abruptly and came to a grinding halt. About two hundred yards down from the road was a long, narrow hollow. Cassie was mystified that there was enough room to accommodate the three shacks perched there.

"Here we are," David explained as he reached for a brown leather satchel and sprang from the rover.

29

Cassie smiled up at David as he opened her door, relieved that the conversation had been interrupted.

The pathway down to the house was strewn with debris, tires, and old car seats. Cassie looked to her right and noticed three old, abandoned cars. When she came closer, she saw several children playing in the cars.

"Shouldn't they be in school?" Cassie asked, puzzled.

David shrugged and answered sadly, "Probably. I've talked to the Browns about it, but they really don't understand how "book larnin" could improve their children's lives. Those are only some of their children. They have eleven."

"Eleven?" asked Cassie in disbelief.

David smiled at the expression on her face. "Yes, and all in three rooms. This area has the highest birth rate in the nation. One of their children is Billy, my patient. He's the I want you to meet."

The couple walked briskly down the path, Cassie slightly in front of David. Sometimes he took her elbow to guide her carefully around the rusting hulk of a large automobile part.

As they neared the house, two russet dogs, lean and muddy, came skulking out from under the high porch which was propped up on rock piers. The dogs hung their heads and growled until David spoke. His voice transformed them magically into a tailwagging welcoming committee.

"I see you must be a frequent visitor," Cassie commented as she released a long breath.

"Always once a week, twice if I can," was his brief reply.

"Howdy, doc, come on in. Billy's waiting for ya," said a friendly voice just inside the slightly open door.

Cassie and David entered the room, squinting until their eyes adjusted to the darkness. One small window gave the room its only light. Three large, iron beds filled the room. Colorful patchwork quilts gave some relief to the stark interior.

"Jesse Brown, this is Pop's Cassie Delaney. She writes for a magazine, and I wanted Billy to meet her. Do you mind if I give Billy a couple of more books to read?" David said after he had made the introduction.

The man, small and unshaven, sat in a straight chair by the fire. Cassie noticed his unhealthy color, and winced inwardly as he went into a spasm of deep rasping coughs.

When the coughing ended, Jesse hoarsely said to the doctor, "Naw, I don't mind. Seems like Billy's a lot happier since ya been comin' around. I didn't see it yur way at first, but seems like ya might be right 'bout him and larnin'—and Miss Delaney's mighty welcome."

"Thank you, Jesse. Sounds like you forgot to take your cough medicine. We'll just go in and see Billy now," the doctor announced.

David led the way to the room on the right where there were three more iron beds. The room had one window and one naked lightbulb hanging from the ceiling, but little warmth or illumination. Cassie shivered as she approached the bed in the corner next to the window.

Her eyes widened in surprise at the sight of a frail boy in his early teens, so deeply engrossed in a book that he had not heard them enter.

"Billy," David spoke his name softly and the youth lifted his eyes, startled.

"Oh, Doc Dave," he exclaimed with such obvious delight that his whole face seemed to light up. "Is this her?"

"You bet, Billy. This is my friend, Miss Delaney, and she's a writer, too," David said.

Cassie looked puzzled. She didn't understand what he meant by "a writer, too."

David answered her unasked question with a smile and said, "Billy is a writer. I'd like for you to see what he's written."

"I'd like to. What have you written, Billy?" she ventured.

"Well, when I got sick last summer, the doc and me got to talkin' about what I could do while I had to stay in bed gettin' over this here fever that bothered my heart some. So he brought me some books. Well, first I read *Tom Sawyer*, and now I'm readin' *Huck Finn*. It's been just like being down on that Mississippi River. I got to thinking about some of the people I know and the little critters up here on this mountain, and I started to write me some stories about them. Seems like when I'm readin' and writin' it's just a little while 'twixt daylight and dark. I don't hardly mind this bed so much," Billy finished with a shy smile.

"That's right, Cassie. This young man has just about read me out of books. My library is getting low. Not only that, but I sent one of his stories to the *Appalachian Chronicle* and they published it!" David added with obvious pride in his patient.

"Yes sir-ree. They give me one hundred dollars for that and was my pa tickled. Bought groceries for a month. He didn't much like me doing this at first 'cause we got into it last year about me wanting to go to school when he wanted me to stay home and work, but he understands better now," Billy Brown explained, his frail countenance lit with excitement.

David put his bag on the floor and sat down on the bed with Billy. "Well, Billy, let me hear your ticker," he said as he took out his stethoscope.

"Sounds much improved, Billy. I believe you'll be able to start getting up a little in about three more weeks, but you have to be careful not to overdo it," David commented as he carefully examined the boy. "Now here are some more books, and I brought you a surprise."

"Oh, thank ya, Doc," the boy exclaimed as David handed him a box of pens and a leather-bound notebook.

"That's for your writing, Billy. It's small enough to take with you when you're able to go out, and here are some larger tablets for your stories. Try to have one ready for me next week, and we'll go over it," David said as he closed his bag and stood up.

Something within Cassie Delaney responded to the youngster and she added, "Billy, it was good to meet you. I wish you could come to my place for a visit when we could have more time to talk."

She felt rather than saw David's approval at her response, and it pleased her. However, her invitation was for her own sake, not for the doctor's. The boy had stirred memories of earlier days when she had had that driving desire to write. Somewhere along the way she had exchanged it for the quest for fame. She longed to recapture the thrill of creating a story—and maybe, vicariously, she could. She enjoyed being an editor, but she really missed the excitement of interviewing people and putting their lives, actions, and emotions on paper.

As they walked back toward the rover, Cassie was lost in her own world of thought. She found herself experiencing mixed emotions. Everything she had seen this afternoon warmed her heart. Pop was right—David was a good man—but, more than that, she envied the sense of purpose and satisfaction that he seemed to posses. It was something that had eluded her for so long.

When David had expertly maneuvered the rover back onto the roadway, he interrupted Cassie's thoughts. "Do you have time to make one more stop?" David asked.

"Another patient?"

"No, just a beautiful view. We passed it on the way up here, but I think you had your eyes closed! It was right after you noticed that steep drop!"

Cassie smiled weakly. "I might have...but I believe I'm getting my mountain legs now. By all means let's not miss that view," she said with more confidence than she felt.

They had not traveled far before David carefully parked the rover on the only level patch of ground and set the brake. Getting out, he quickly walked to Cassie's side and helped her out.

"I've traveled these mountains often over the last three years, but I have never found anything to surpass this view," he declared as they stood above the great spectacle of wooded hills and valleys spread before them.

The intensity of color was even more dynamic in the late afternoon light. The low-hanging sun splashed vibrant pinks and lavenders in the sky above the collage of color in the valleys far below. Although it was still light, a full moon could be seen clearly in the late afternoon sky. The air was crisp and cool. Gentle smoke wafted upward from houses, which, from their vantage point, resembled children's toys.

Entranced by the view, Cassandra unconsciously took a step forward and immediately felt David's strong hand on her shoulders in a protective grasp. "Better not venture any farther than you are. I'd really hate to lose you to the view," he quipped as his hands relaxed their grip but continued to rest lightly upon her shoulder.

Cassie tried in vain to think of a clever response, but his nearness disturbed her. "David," Cassie said his name evenly as she glanced at him over her shoulder. "Do you think the large granite rock over there would be a safe spot to enjoy the view?"

David flashed his crooked grin as he dropped his hands from her shoulders. "That was placed here especially for sightseers, children, and people who just like to sit and think."

They walked toward the massive piece of granite which was larger than the house they had just left. Its highest point was about twenty feet, and from there it gradually descended into four different tiers. The overall surface was smooth and gently sloped, which made climbing an easy task. The lowest tier of the surface was wide and flat like a predesigned bench.

Cassie stood before the mammoth rock formation and carefully examined its many dimensions. "Beat you to the top!" she exclaimed, and she was off before she had finished speaking. David stood there briefly before he accepted the challenge. He watched with pleasure as the dark-haired form moved gracefully up the granite surface. Then, responding with almost boyish eagerness, he yelled, "You're on!"

Cassie had a good head start, but she was no match for his agility and long strides. He passed her a few feet from the top and turned to pull her up the final few steps.

"Well," she said breathlessly, "I almost beat you."

"Maybe next time, you will. You were at a disadvantage in those boots." He smiled at her flushed face and sparkling eyes.

"Doctor, you're being gallant. You failed to mention the head start I had on you. I'm really out of practice. It's been years since I've climbed any trees or scampered up rocks," she admitted as she casually dropped his hand and walked carefully toward the front of the granite to get a clearer view of the valley below.

"It's so beautiful in the fall," she observed. "Grandmother said this time of year was a 'symphony of color.' It's hard to believe that, mixed with all this beauty, are poor families like we saw today. How can they bear to live like that?" Cassie asked with heartfelt concern.

David stood beside her. "They really don't have much choice. Jobs are scarce, the people are uneducated, and this is all most of them have ever known. There are ways they do need help, but most of these families have a special bond and closeness that many would envy."

"I guess you know them pretty well. How many patients do you have?"

"I started off with five or six a month when I first came. No one trusted me until Pop helped me break the

35

ice. Now, when winter gets here, and illness really comes to the mountains, I see nearly a hundred a month in the ninety-mile radius I travel."

Cassie looked up into his clear blue eyes inquisitively. "David, you sound like a country doctor of bygone years—making his rounds to see his patients—but what happens to them if you decide to leave?"

"I'm not going to leave," he stated firmly. "My life is here and, God willing, I'll have help and a clinic one day."

"I admire your dedication, but I must confess I don't see how you can be happy spending the rest of your life here."

David laughed, "You'd be surprised how many times I've been asked that question...but I've found that happiness comes not so much from where you are, but from what you're doing and..." He looked directly into her eyes and quietly added, "who you're with."

Cassie felt a warm flush on her face as David said those last words, but she could not look away from the tenderness in his magnetic blue eyes. The silence was heavy between them. Finally, David took her hand and said, "We'd better be going. It won't be long before dark falls, and the driving is much easier with even a little daylight."

Cassie followed obediently, again surprised at her schoolgirl reactions. *What is wrong with me?* she thought. *Why does this country doctor affect me so?*

Once again inside the rover, Cassie began to feel more like herself as they cautiously plodded back down the mountain. She was still aware of the doctor's presence, but her face was no longer flushed, and her heartbeat had returned to normal.

It wasn't long before they arrived on the main road and were approaching Delaney Farms. David had been right: the darkness had fallen quickly.

"Well, Miss Delaney, here you are safe and sound," David said as he walked with her to the house.

"Thanks for inviting me. It was enlightening...and I *would* like to read Billy's stories."

He reached for the keys she was holding and unlocked her front door. "I'm glad you could come. Ride with me again sometime—and, as for Billy, you've made one mountain boy very happy."

David returned her keys as she walked in the front door. Cassie turned to say goodnight but did not speak when she saw the same look in his eyes that had been there as they stood facing each other on the massive rock.

"Cassie," was all he said as he gently brushed her cheek with his fingers and turned to walk away.

Cassie stood in the doorway and watched as he cranked up the rover and slowly drove into the night.

"Pop," Cassie said weakly as she waved good-by. "He's just...not my type."

Chapter Four

The day dawned cold and gray in Manhattan. The winds that swirled around the lofty Hamilton Towers, which housed the offices of *Woman's Life* magazine, had a biting edge unusual for so early in October.

Tony Hamilton Saikas, the magazine's owner and publisher, sat at his desk and stared morosely out his eastern window at a dawn that wasn't there. Heavy clouds obscured the pink-tinged sky of a new day.

Tony hadn't gone home the night before. In fact, he hadn't been home for several nights. His only sleep had consisted of a few restless hours spent on the designer sofa that graced his penthouse office.

The dark circles under his eyes were the only telltale signs that he hadn't rested well. He was immaculately dressed as always. The beige cashmere jacket and matching pants had been taken from a well-stocked closet in his dressing room suite.

The shower and shave had refreshed his body, but his weariness went deeper. He had a pain that gnawed inside and threatened to destroy him. He didn't go home at night because the halls and silent rooms of his palatial mansion echoed the emptiness inside him.

He had bought the house *for her* because she had seen it and loved it, but she had rejected his gift and, with it, him. *Why?* He didn't understand her talk about a "lifetime commitment." How could he know what or whom he'd want ten years from now?

Remembering their last quarrel, he angrily muttered into the oppressive half-light of the mute office, "Who does she think she is, anyway—and what has she done to my life?"

With a heaviness in his step, he walked to his massive desk of inlaid mahogany. Reaching the desk, he stood pensively with both hands resting on it. His eyes fell on a photograph in a brushed gold frame placed prominently on his opulent desk. He stared directly into the face of the dark-haired woman, and struggled to control the frustration and anger that flooded his mind.

Suddenly he seized the gold-framed picture and flung it violently across the room. The shattering of glass cut through the early morning silence. His uncontrolled outburst expended, he sat down heavily in his deep leather chair and began to clench and unclench his fists. He did not mind anger. In fact, he felt it could be a positive ally, but only if it were controlled—and he had lost control, again.

His clenched fists gradually relaxed as his anger subsided. Then, with deliberate effort, he got out of the chair and walked over to examine the photograph in the broken frame. It had not been hurt.

Tony stared longingly at the girl in the picture. Her dark brown eyes and beautiful smile seemed to reach out and embrace him, and the Parisian fragrance she so often wore invaded his senses even now.

As he continued to brood over her lovely face, his handsome features again were distorted by a sullen look, and his lips curled tight with tension.

Few people had ever seen this side of Tony Hamilton Saikas. To all those who knew him, or thought they knew him, he was charming—warm, witty, thoughtful and very generous. But beneath his warm exterior beat the heart of a man, calculating and cold. He had learned to use his charm, much as one would use a carefully developed skill. This, plus his money, had always gotten him whatever he wanted, and, to Tony, what he wanted was really the only thing that mattered.

His tension deepened and his square jaws clenched in renewed anger. "You said you wanted a six months' leave to finish your novel and to think. Instead, you disappear—without a word to me!" he heard himself saying aloud. "Cassandra Delaney, no one has ever gotten the best of me and you won't. I will find you. You will be mine!"

Tony's muscular body relaxed as if this verbal declaration somehow had given release. He did not know where she was, but he knew she would be back, and on his terms.

For a moment, his previous weariness seemed to lift visibly. His facial expression lost some of its tautness, and its structural features became more evident. Tony Hamilton Saikas was a handsome man.

The product of a Greek father, who had made his wealth in real estate, and an Irish mother from a wealthy New York family. He had inherited the thick black hair, piercing dark eyes and congenial manner of the Greeks; but his height, muscular frame, and explosive temper were from the Irish. Tony's physical attributes were not the only evidence of parental influence. He was at *Woman's Life* because of his mother.

The magazine had been a gift of sorts from his mother. She was chairman of the board and major stockholder of one of the world's largest publishing corporations. It was a family business, and Tony was the only heir living. Someday his mother's position would be rightfully his, but she was a business genius, aggressive and astute, and she refused to consider turning over her stock or position until he had proven himself in the business world. *Woman's Life* had been his testing ground, and so far, he'd come through with flying colors.

The momentary spark of satisfaction faded as his cold dark eyes looked out across the awakening skyline and his thoughts turned to Cassandra, and the first time they'd met.

Woman's Life magazine had been losing ground for over two years. In a daring business move, Tony had fired the seasoned editor and decided to replace her with a younger woman, one with innovative ideas. Several qualified women had sought the prestigious position, but it was not until he had interviewed Cassandra that he had found all the necessary qualifications.

Tony turned from the window and reached for Cassie's picture as he remembered their interview. He had been sequestered behind his large desk, intently studying the resume of one Cassandra Delaney, shortly before her scheduled appointment.

She was a well-respected journalist; in fact, it was her exposé on the fashion industry that had brought her to his attention, and two words had been used consistently to describe her—workaholic and creative. Her resume was impressive, he had thought, but it would be the interview that determined his choice.

He was still studying her file when his secretary buzzed him to announce, "Ms. Cassandra Delaney." On an impulse, he had left his desk and walked toward the door to greet her. When he looked at her for the first time, his usual composure was briefly shaken. She was not at all what he had expected.

Cassandra Delaney was a vision of feminine loveliness. She was dressed in a linen suit of cranberry red. A softly tailored short jacket gently skimmed her small waistline. She wore no jewelry, except for a small pair of delicate red and gold antique earrings. Her dark hair was pulled back in a chignon, while wisps of curls framed her translucent complexion and gave her a look of sophisticated innocence.

Tony, amazed by her overwhelming beauty, tried vainly to remember her name. She saved him by very graciously extending her hand as she spoke her name in introduction.

Regaining his composure, he took her outstretched hand and smiled warmly while he offered her a nearby chair. With elegant bearing, she sat down and waited as he took his place behind his desk and reached for her resumé. She sat quietly as he again studied her file.

He remembered the tick of the oriental clock as he used the seconds to regain the cool business logic he must have before he could judge this woman's professional merits.

Finally, he looked up and asked in his most charming manner if the things he had heard about her were true.

He remembered her smiling retort, "That depends on what you've heard, Mr. Saikas."

"If you are sent out on a story, you get it, period," he quietly explained.

Smiling with confidence, she nodded her head.

As the interview progressed, he became more impressed with Cassandra Delaney, the journalist. He knew that her beauty and personal poise would be an asset as editor, but it was her determination that influenced his decision.

His business wisdom told him that, if she were editor, *Woman's Life* would consume her. It was for this that he hired her.

Tony had made the right choice. Within three years, with Cassie's persistence and innovative ideas, *Woman's Life* had become the number-one magazine read by American women.

His handsome features looked uncharacteristically sentimental as he thought of their beginning relationship. At first, it had been all business, totally professional. An employer-employee relationship, held together by a common goal—making *Woman's Life* number one.

But, as the months had passed, the magazine had brought them constantly together—at the office, at meetings, at parties—and he had begun to see her not only as his successful editor, but as an enchanting woman. He desired her, but, despite all of his tried-and-true methods, she retained her professional aloofness.

Tony shook his head, remembering the frustration this had caused him. She was a challenge and a paradox at the same time. He knew she wanted success and everything that went with it—and, through him, it was within her reach. Yet, consistently, she thwarted his advances.

Although she still remained a mystery, he had accepted the challenge. Throwing caution to the wind, he had decided to "court" her in the old fashioned way.

Tony sighed deeply as he thought of the picnics in the country. Even now he hardly could believe that he had taken off afternoons from work to go on picnics! Yet, he still could close his eyes and feel the late spring sun and the contentment he had had on those occasions. He could see the look in Cassie's eyes as he had picked flowers in the field and brought them to her.

When they had gone horseback riding in Central Park, he had marveled at her grace and horsemanship. He had sent her candy and flowers and even taken her to his parents' home on several occasions.

Gradually, the successful career woman, who had not taken time for a personal life, had responded to his attention; and, to his delight, her aloofness disappeared like freshly fallen snow under the warm rays of the sun.

He could not possess her totally, but her tender kisses and warm embraces were enough until he could claim her entirely.

He had thought he'd won when she finally had said, "I love you, Tony," but he hadn't. She wanted a lifetime commitment and not just the live-in relationship which he had offered. The pressure returned to his chest and, once again, an undefinable feeling gnawed at his gut. Could he have been wrong? He hadn't really understood how much Cassandra differed from other ambitious females. He had thought only her game plan was different. Evidently, her sense of values was deeper than he realized.

He thumbed through a file absently as he remembered the last time he had seen her. The hurt in her eyes had been genuine. Her tears had been real when he had told her that he loved her and wanted her—but he couldn't make the kind of commitment she had described.

"What if I *did* marry you? Maybe...just maybe..." He said to the picture now lying on his desk. "Cassandra, soon I'll know where you are...and then I'll watch...and wait."

Chapter Five

The dissonant ring of the telephone woke Cassie from a deep and dreamless sleep. She struggled to consciousness and managed a sleepy "Hello."

She thought she was still dreaming as she heard a familiar voice say, "Hello, Darling. I've missed you."

Awake or asleep, she recognized the voice of Tony Hamilton Saikas, and was so stunned that for a moment she could not answer.

Once again the voice spoke, this time not so pleasantly. "Cassandra, this is Tony—or have you forgotten my voice so soon?"

Fully awake now, Cassie coolly replied into the receiver, "No, Tony, I could hardly forget your voice. I was asleep and surprised, that's all."

"Still asleep, my love? Beauty sleep or a wild night out?" he questioned, undaunted by her coolness.

"There is a time difference here, you know. Anyway, it's early, even in New York," she retorted.

"You avoided my question."

"I really don't think it's any of your business how late my night was," she replied, as irritation began to sound in her voice.

"You haven't always felt that way, darling. I can remember when your life was my business—"

"That is in the past, Tony, and better forgotten," Cassie quickly interrupted. "Anyway, how did you find me?"

"It wasn't easy," Tony admitted. "Why did you leave without telling me where I could find you? Were you trying to hide from me, Cassandra?"

"Why should I try to hide from you?"

"That's what I would like to know." Tony's voice, normally so pleasant, had taken on an edge that surprised Cassie.

"I don't know what you're talking about," she countered. "I'm here to finish my book as we agreed, and my six months aren't up yet."

"I know what our agreement was, but it didn't include your disappearing on me without a word. I don't like that. By the way, how is the book coming?" he asked.

"It's coming along," Cassie hedged.

"That's good. Do you think you could shorten your leave to four months instead of six? Things are going well here, but the board is beginning to ask me questions that I can't answer. Mostly about you." Tony's voice had recovered some of its persuasive smoothness.

"No, I don't see any way that I can shorten my stay. You promised me six months and six months I want!" Cassie answered, more heatedly than she had intended.

"I know that, Cassandra, but you didn't tell me you were going to be out of touch for all that time. What if a crisis comes up at the magazine? Doesn't what you have accomplished here mean anything to you anymore? Doesn't what *we had* mean anything to you anymore?" The old Tony finally had gained control and he used his most charming manner on her.

"Yes, Tony, the magazine is still very important to me. As for what we meant to each other, that's in the past. You're just my employer—one who has given me a six-month leave of absence. There was no stipulation that I had to check in periodically. Isn't Hilary taking care of things satisfactorily?"

"Yes, Hilary is doing a superb job—maybe too good. I'd be a little concerned if I were you; you know your contract runs out in April." Cassie did not miss the threatening hint in his voice.

"I'm glad that she's doing so well. What you do with my contract in April is your business," she responded without a trace of fear.

"But what about *me*, Cassie? Only you can fill that void," Tony crooned.

"That won't work with me anymore. Your needs and mine are worlds apart, and I don't want that pain again," Cassie replied emphatically.

"I know, sweetheart, but it needn't be that way. Just say the word, and everything I have will be at your feet."

"Everything but your name, Tony. Remember? It wasn't your possessions that I wanted; it was a lifetime commitment. You know, one with a gold band and a death-us-do-part promise?" Cassie ended her statement weakly as bitter memories threatened to overcome her.

Tony paused before he quietly said, "I know, I know, but I've been giving that some thought. When you come back, Cassandra, you might find a different Tony, one not quite as opposed to your conditions."

"I don't think that would make any difference now. What we had is in the past, and I think I would rather it stay that way," Cassie said with quiet finality.

A stunned Tony Saikas answered, "You'll be back. You and I are alike; you know that you want what I want; you'd never be happy without the power and prestige of a successful career. I'm not worried. I'll see you soon, here in New York. Until then, I'll miss you." With that the line went dead.

Cassie was visibly shaken by the call. Her face was ashen white as she stumbled from the large old bed. Tony's veiled threats did not frighten her. She recognized them for what they were: his enormous vanity. What had unnerved her was his assessment of her character. *Was she like him?*

"Oh, God," she breathed, "don't let it be so."

As the golden days of October had passed, Cassie had experienced an emotional release that she hadn't felt in months. David's occasional visits had helped her to push aside painful memories. Several times he had brought articles that Billy had written. They had read them together and marveled at the sensitivity in one so young.

Almost before she realized it, the horses had exchanged their sleek coats for winter ones and, as the trees shed their fall leaves to become bare branches, her heart had shed part of its bitterness, or so she thought.

Now Tony's call brought her face to face with some disturbing facts. She had come to Kentucky to sort out her life and to finish her novel. Thus far she had done neither.

The painful soul-searching that she had pushed aside returned with vigor, and she knew that soon she must face her options and decide the course her life was to take. Tony's assessment of her was a bitter pill to swallow; now she must find the truth about herself and choose accordingly.

So on this November day full of blustery rain and falling temperatures, Cassie pulled the four chapters she had written in New York from her briefcase, and went to work.

She had started a mystery about the world of high fashion, but the manuscript had lost all of its intrigue for her. As she reread it, the characters seemed like wooden images chasing silly dreams. *Why don't my characters have depth*? she questioned. She knew intimately the nature of the people she was writing about. She knew their lifestyle, their values; yet her book seemed shallow, the characters' goals and ambitions empty. Doggedly, she forged on, with her cardboard characters, voicing their hollow phrases, filling the empty pages.

As her frustration and self-doubt mounted, the cold, gloomy days of November gave way to the wintry ones of December. Her daily visits with Pop were the only relief from her self-imposed isolation. The cold weather had brought a flurry of sickness to the mountains, and Cassie saw David only once a week when he made his routine stop to check on Aubry. Today she even had refused to go to town with Pop on the weekly buying trip.

But that evening, Cassie grew tired of her isolation and invited Pop to supper. As he brought her news from town and told her new stories of her grandparents' struggles, she found herself strangely comforted. Cassie wondered if she might find some of the answers for which she searched in the knowledge of her heritage.

After supper, she set up the checker board by a roaring fire in the old stone fireplace, and, just as they sat down to play, the doorbell rang.

It was David, and, seeing the delight in Pop's eyes, Cassie relinquished her checkers to the doctor and curled up in a soft chair by the fire with a classic culled from her grandfather's library.

However, she found it difficult to concentrate on the book in her hand as she observed the two men so engrossed in their game. Surprisingly, she found herself comparing David with Tony!

She was noting David's rugged good looks. His manner of dress was so different from the designer suits Tony wore; yet David wore his jeans and split suede jacket with a natural grace and sense of worth that communicated itself in the way he walked and looked. Although Cassie had never seen him in anything but casual wear, she knew intuitively that he would be equally at ease in formal clothes.

Cassie was curious about David's sense of purpose. She knew that it was anchored in his work, or "his calling," as he described it. He was so certain that he was doing what God wanted him to do with his life. It must be this knowledge that gave David his quiet confidence and strength, she reasoned. He had a contentment and joy in his work that the wealthiest men she'd ever known did not have. It was a mystery to Cassie, one that really intrigued her.

Cassie must have been staring into the fire for several minutes when David startled her by saying, "A penny for your thoughts."

She looked up and noticed that the game had ended. She answered honestly, "I was thinking about you, doctor."

He grinned at her candor and remarked, "I'm flattered. What in particular were you thinking?"

"I was curious about your work and what you find so satisfying up in those hills," she replied as Pop listened intently.

"That's hard to explain. What do you find so satisfying about your writing?" he asked, deftly turning the question.

Cassie thought for a moment, and then said, "At this point, nothing."

"Why?" the doctor probed.

"The people in my book don't really seem to live."

"Then write about real people."

When Cassie heard his simple statement, a look of revelation broke across her face. "Doctor, you just cured a deep state of depression with this house call!" Laughing at David's puzzled look, she explained, "I know what's wrong with my book. It's the wrong one!"

"What do you mean?" he asked, bewildered.

"Simply this, doctor: how would you like to be a hero in my new book?" she laughed.

"You're flattering me again, but I'm not the stuff heroes are made of."

"That's a matter of opinion, but, anyway, aren't heroes larger than life?" she teased.

"Maybe so, but, seriously, what are you babbling about?" he asked.

"I don't know if I can explain, but I've just decided to discard my manuscript and start over. I'm going to start right where I am, with the people I've met here, and the ones I've heard about." Cassie jumped up from the chair. "Oh, David, Pop, it can be something of value, real value."

Cassie's oval face was aglow with excitement, and her dark eyes shone. Pop and David both looked astonished and relieved at her transformation. Gone was the furrowed brow, and the shoulders that had sagged in despondency were once again straight and proud. She had found one of the answers for which she was searching—a meaningful work into which she could put her whole heart.

Cassie exchanged her despondency for a new zest for life as the creative energy dormant within her flowed once more.

Even though daylight came late and left early, Cassie's work day was long. She was eager to get up in the morning and reluctant to leave her typewriter at night.

Before the week was over, she had outlined a novel, using the hills and hollows of nineteenth-century Kentucky as a backdrop. The main character was a pioneer physician whose love for the land and the people was deep and abiding. Cassie masterfully blended the qualities she had remembered and heard about in her grandfather with those she had observed in David McBride—shaping a hero who would be strong and appealing.

With the outline and main character sketch completed, Cassie abandoned her typewriter in favor of trips to town to talk to the local people as she researched the remaining characters and events.

Usually she went alone, but occasionally David drove her, and along the way she would question him at length about the mannerisms and customs of his patients. He was amused at first with Cassie's child-like excitement and curiosity, but, as the visits progressed, he too became excited about the idea of portraying the

51

spirit of 'his people' on the written page.

Once Cassie had captured the doctor's imagination, he dropped by several nights each week to share anecdotes and new insights about the people whose lives she would chronicle.

It was during these times of shared companionship that Cassie began to admit to herself how strongly she was attracted to the doctor. She looked forward to his visits excitedly—and the valuable information that he brought was not the main reason.

The month of November evaporated in a flurry of work.

Cassie began the actual writing of her book and was progressing rapidly. The weeks following Thanksgiving ushered in an early winter, and with it a wave of sickness which brought an end to David's weekly visits. Pop came down with a cold, so Cassie's only interruptions were her chores and carrying Pop meals once or twice a day.

Although the book was going better than she could have hoped, Cassie still felt vaguely dissatisfied. One afternoon, as the clouds hung low and more snow threatened, she got up from her typewriter and wandered restlessly to the window.

She saw the branches of the trees heavy with snow from yesterday's storm. The bleakness of the winterscape matched her mood. *What is wrong with me?* she thought. *I know this book is good. I know it will be a work with meaning, so why do I feel like this? Is it because I miss Tony? No. Come to think of it, I haven't thought of him in days. Could it be that I miss David? That's true, I have missed him, but it's something more than that. I thought when I settled this thing about my book everything would be all right; yet, something is still not quite right.*

That evening Cassie abandoned her writing for a night. After a long, warm bath she dressed in tweed slacks and a bright red turtleneck. Just as she settled down by the fire to read, the doorbell rang. Opening the door, she saw, to her delight, David standing there with a chess set under his arm.

"Well, come in, good doctor. What have you there?" she asked.

"Something to stretch your brain and challenge your mind," he said in mock seriousness.

"What?" she asked, mimicking his tone. "Does my mind need challenging?"

"Maybe a little. Anyway, I'd like some of your valuable time all to myself," he added casually.

The declaration took Cassie by surprise. Quickly taking the box from him, she tried to cover her confusion. "Pop won't be here tonight. He's staying in with his cold."

"I know, Cassie. That's why I'm here."

A smile of pleasure spread over her face, but no reply came immediately to mind. She turned to lead the way to the study.

The couple walked over to the game table in the corner near the fireplace and carefully removed Pop's checker board to make room for their chess game.

"Careful, you'll dislodge those bottle caps from the board," David warned.

"Don't worry, doctor," Cassie laughed. "I'd have to leave Kentucky permanently if I lost one of his men."

"Has Pop ever said why he won't use regular checkers?"

"He said if he got any of those 'new-fangled' ones he'd lose his touch. He's used this same set for thirty years. I bought him a nice set when I first came back, but he made me take them back to the store and swap them for horse feed!" Cassie exclaimed, with her hands on her hips and her eyes twinkling with merriment. All traces of her former restlessness were gone.

David chuckled softly as he ran a finger caressingly

over the worn board. "That Aubry does have a mind of his own."

"Yes, but it's chock-full of wisdom."

"I know. He's helped me through some rough spots and his advice was always right on target," David responded with a slight frown.

"You've had some rough spots, Dr. McBride?" Cassie asked casually.

"One or two, but don't get me to confess. It might spoil my image," David teased, his frown gone.

"No danger of that," was Cassie's too-quick response.

David looked at her and raised his eyebrows questioningly.

Cassie paused for a moment before laughing up at him, "We're all friends here, David. You don't have to maintain an image."

"That's a relief, because I'm no good at image making. No, what you see is what you get. Now then, do you think our friendship is strong enough to survive if I give you a good thrashing in a game of chess?"

"Probably, but don't you count on winning, because I 'ain't no slouch' when it comes to this game," she drawled laughingly.

"Sounds like I've got my work cut out for me, Ms. Delaney." With a slight bow, he pulled a chair out for her.

The two played long into the evening as they became engrossed in the complicated game. David finally defeated Cassie shortly after midnight and demanded an early-morning breakfast as his prize.

Laughing together, they made their way into the kitchen. With David watching her intently, she quickly whipped up a meal of bacon and eggs.

"Let's eat in front of the fire," Cassie suggested as she picked up a tray.

"That sounds just right." He took the tray from her.

Cassie became acutely aware of David's nearness as she looked up into his deep blue eyes. For a moment, the impulse to reach up and caress his cheek overwhelmed her. The look in his eyes seemed to recognize her nearness as well, and their bantering friendliness evaporated.

Cassie lowered her eyes and turned to leave the kitchen. Carrying the tray, David followed and set their food down on a low table between the fire and a chintz-covered loveseat.

They took their plates in their laps, sat on the floor, and ate in silence. Suddenly David asked, "What are your plans for the future?"

"I don't know. I guess it'll be back to *Woman's Life*," she said quietly.

"I see," he responded and dropped his questioning.

After they had finished their food, David looked at his watch and rose to his feet. "All good things must come to an end and so must this visit, Cassie."

"Must you go?" she asked, as his impressive frame towered over her.

"I really must," he emphasized. Somehow she felt he meant something more than the hour's lateness.

He extended his hand and helped her up. "See me to the door, beautiful lady," he said lightly.

As they walked to the door, David did not relinquish her hand. The firelight danced across the room. At the door he turned and looked at her intently as the warm glow from the fire bathed her in radiance.

"Don't make your decision to go back too hastily, Cassie. There could be a life for you here, you know. One infinitely more satisfying." With that, he took her hand and gently raised it to his lips.

Once again, Cassie stared in startled silence as David disappeared through the massive old front door.

Chapter Six

Cassie's writing continued to progress rapidly. When the weather broke, she and Pop made their way into town—and, to their amazement, it blazed with colored lights and shiny tinsel. Carols chimed from the local church, and shops were adorned with bright red and green decorations.

Cassie had been so busy that she had forgotten Christmas was so near. Perhaps she had subconsciously pushed it to the back of her mind. Holidays had been times of sadness for her since the death of her grandparents.

Usually they had been spent alone or at meaningless parties; but, in the town today, she recalled some of the thrill she had felt as a small child when her parents had taken her to this same village, and she had picked out the doll she wanted, and later a bicycle.

She remembered how excited she used to be on Christmas Eve as the Delaneys would trim the tree, one cut from her granddad's woods. Then they would go to church to see the manger scene in the yard outside and hear the story of the Christ Child.

Cassie wondered aloud, "Do you suppose the manger scene is still there?"

She could not suppress her curiosity, so she walked to the end of the street—and there, just outside the building, was the same scene—Mary, Joseph, and the Baby Jesus, with the animals looking on in mute admiration.

Unbidden tears of longing brimmed in Cassie's eyes as she remembered the wonderful holidays so long ago. She yearned to recapture some of that joy today.

Those memories were a stark contrast to the lonely ones of her college days when she had had to work through the holidays for the next semester's tuition.

Her memories startled her into the realization that Pop, too, must have been lonely after her family was gone. It pained her that the years she had been able to *afford* to come home, she *hadn't*. She had convinced herself that an expensive gift to him would suffice.

Who knew better than Cassie that an expensive gift *wouldn't* suffice? A vivid picture of last Christmas flashed in her mind.

Tony had taken her to an intimate restaurant on Christmas Eve. Cassie could remember how thrilled she had been when he had pulled a small velvet box from his pocket and opened it. Inside had been a large emerald ring, perfect in its deep green hue and clarity, a stone of exceptional value. He had slipped it on her finger and whispered, "For the woman I want in my life; Merry Christmas."

They had left the restaurant and sped through the night in his powerful automobile, with its low whine of the motor and soft, leather seats. She could recall the warmth of the car inside as she noted the snow piled high on each side of the street, where the snow plows had been busy clearing the New York City thoroughfares.

If someone had asked her that night if she were happy, she would have said deliriously so, but, in retrospect, was she? Cassie had thought that the exquisite ring and Tony's words had been the promise of a beginning commitment. Then, when he had given her the palatial house in August, she had been sure he wanted to marry her. He hadn't. The ring, the house, and his words all had been a sham.

Tony Saikas had wanted her to share his life, all right—a life without commitment. She had given him back the emerald ring and told him to keep his house.

He had been shocked—and angry. Never before had he made any woman an offer like that. He couldn't believe her, let alone understand her!

Come to think of it, Cassie didn't understand it herself. She had not been playing coy with Tony; she had believed he loved her, and, for some reason, to her, love meant marriage. She guessed that it had something to do with this place, her people, her upbringing, maybe even God.

For the first time since her college days, Cassie had a strong desire to go to church on Christmas Eve. She made plans right then that she and Pop would have a Christmas to remember. One like those that had made her so happy as a child.

When Christmas Eve dawned, the sky was an unblemished blue, and the sun sparkled on the newfallen snow. Outside the house, the branches were covered with ice, and the evergreens bowed under their load of white. Inside, the fragrance of cedar from a freshly-cut tree in the study permeated the rooms. There were boughs of holly over the mantle, and the aromas of freshly-baked gingerbread and ham filled the rooms.

Cassie had taken an afternoon off from her writing to do some baking. The overcoat and hat that she had bought for Pop in town were wrapped and under the tree, as well as a pair of warm, leather gloves for David. The physician had planned to go to church with them that evening; they were going to open their gifts and eat the Christmas dinner before church.

Cassie's day was busy and, before she could believe it possible, the shadows were lengthening and it was almost time for dinner.

When she realized the time, Cassie ran upstairs to freshen up. As she ran a comb through her curls and touched her lips with color, she surveyed her image in the mirror. She had on a red sweater-dress with no jewelry. The choice was perfect. The vivid color set off her striking features, and the excitement of the day made her eyes bright. Pleased with the effect, she turned to go back downstairs just as she heard David ring the doorbell.

David entered with two gaily-wrapped gifts in his hands and a bouquet of red roses!

"David, where on earth did you get roses this time of the year?" she exclaimed in obvious delight.

"Well, ma'am, when you're an important man like me, you pull certain strings and find just about anything you want. Especially if you know the local florist, and you made a house call to him at two o'clock this morning," he teased.

"Whatever your connections, David, I do appreciate these beauties," she returned with a soft smile.

"Smells like my grandmother's house at Christmas," David commented as he took a deep breath.

"I hoped it would; that's just the way I wanted it to be—not your grandmother's, but mine. I really had a hard time following her recipes; mostly it was a pinch of this and a pinch of that so I hope it's edible."

"What I want to know is where is Pop and where is the mistletoe?" He grinned mischievously.

"Why, Doctor, you'd better behave yourself. Pop's in the kitchen carving the ham, and will spring to my defense on a moment's notice. Anyway, dinner's ready. Church starts in two hours, so we'll have time for a leisurely meal," she added, as she felt a blush of pleasure rise to her already flushed cheeks.

Pop announced dinner and the three sat down to a bountiful table of food. The table was covered with a red cloth and the Delaney china and crystal glistened in the candlelight. Pop said a prayer of thanksgiving, and then they ate their food hungrily while enjoying warm conversation. Cassie felt an unusual contentment as she recognized in this simple pleasure a link to her past. To her it seemed almost like a homecoming from a distant journey. She couldn't explain the feeling, but she relished it.

After Christmas dinner, they opened their gifts. Pop opened his presents and discovered a down jacket from David and the overcoat and hat from Cassie. He said, "Ya shore don't want a fella to get cold, do ya? I shore do like them, but they're too purty to wear to work in."

"That's exactly what you're supposed to do with that jacket. We don't want any more of that bronchitis. You can save your coat for church," the doctor said firmly.

David was pleased with his gloves from Cassie and chuckled when he opened a box of shotgun shells from Pop. "You trying to tell me something, Aubry?"

"Yup, ya need to take off from work a spell and hunt a bit. Besides, I sorta been hankering for some good bird meat," he answered wryly.

Cassie was surprised to find that David had given her a down jacket, too, and Pop had given her some warm, fur-lined boots. "You men must want to keep me warm. I really do like them," she declared.

"Seems like a fancy-dressing lass like you needs some good warm clothes for the out-of-doors, especially if you plan to go on more calls with me," David explained.

Soon the wrapping paper was cleared away and the trio left for church.

They arrived just as the last worshipers were being seated. Cassie felt the warm spirit reflected on the faces, many of them now familiar, around her.

The service was brief, but very moving. The pastor read the Christmas story from the Gospel of Luke and then offered a brief sermon on the significance of Christ's birth. The same peace which the angel proclaimed that night in Bethlehem, the pastor assured them, was still available to all through Jesus Christ, God's Son.

The service ended with the stirring strains of "Joy To the World." Cassie looked around her and saw radiant faces singing the wondrous message. Then she, too, began to sing, as tears stung her eyes and a deep longing filled her heart.

Winter finally released its hold and, with warmer weather heralding spring, Cassie threw herself into completing her novel. Busy days at the typewriter were interrupted only by necessary chores. She took a brisk ride in the mornings and evenings to exercise her horses and herself.

One day, David came back from his rounds early and dropped by the house just as she and Pop were saddling Nadia for her evening ride.

"Why don't ya ride Shebazzi, Doc? I bet Cassie'd like the company," the old man suggested.

"Well, Pop, I think that's what I'd like to do. How about it, Cassie?" David asked in his soft drawl.

"Do you think you can keep up with me?" teased Cassie.

"What do you mean, woman? Don't you know I was born in the saddle?" the doctor retorted. "You'll have a hard time keeping up with *me!*"

It was an exhilarating day. With a cold nip in the air despite the bright mid-afternoon sun. The horses were prancing and eager for a run.

The couple guided the horses toward a level stretch of ground where a wide trail wandered through the woods. The pounding of hooves as the horses expended their pent-up energy precluded conversation, so the two riders gave themselves to the magnificient rhythm of horse and rider. Cassie was an expert horsewoman, but her expertise did not exceed David's. When they finally slowed the horses to a gallop, the doctor was slightly ahead of Cassie, and she had time to marvel at his ease and management of the flashy stallion. Horse and rider seemed made for each other, and she was impressed by the controlled power they both conveyed.

Cassie and David arrived back at the house with red cheeks and bright eyes. As the couple dismounted, Aubry shooed them on to the house, promising to care for the horses.

"David, I'm impressed. Do you have horses?" Cassie asked.

"Not at the moment. I have a big empty barn and would like to get some, but right now my budget and time won't allow it. How is it a city girl like you has two fine animals like these?" he questioned.

"I kept Nadia at a stable in Connecticut, and occasionally I'd get to ride her on weekends. Then I decided to bring her back to Kentucky for Pop to look after, and he suggested that we buy a stallion to start our own herd. I looked into the possibilities and decided it would be a good venture for both of us. We plan to breed Nadia in May, so we should have our first foal the following April. I was advised it could be a good investment for me, but I really did it more for Pop. He taught me everything I know about the care of animals," Cassie explained.

The tender look in Cassie's eyes prompted David to ask, "Pop means a lot to you, doesn't he?"

"More than I realized. He's all the family I have and he's not really family. He has no one either. It pains me to think how I kept out of touch all those years, but it won't happen again," she said with quiet resolution.

They warmed themselves in front of the fire in the large library that she used for her office. Soon the two of them were laughing together over steaming mugs of spiced apple cider. As they sat facing each other in soft brown leather chairs that had belonged to Cassie's grandfather, David entertained her with more stories of his adventures among the mountain folk.

She had a moment of nostalgia as she envisioned her grandparents sharing similar moments in pleasant conversation, and sitting in these same chairs in this very room.

Gently David set his cup down and said, "I've enjoyed this afternoon more than you can know. I hate to end it, but I've got to go. You know, each time I see you I enjoy it more. May I ride with you again?"

"Anytime, you know that," she said as he turned to go.

When he reached the door, he hesitated and turned to look at her as she stood by the fire, one hand resting on the mantle. His eyes seemed to drink in her beauty, the lovely eyes bright from the brisk ride and stimulating conversation, the tendrils of dark curls caressing her forehead.

Cassie's heart skipped a beat as she recognized the unmistakable look of desire in his eyes, but with that look was one of tenderness and something else she couldn't quite define. She watched, entranced, as he struggled with his emotions that were, for a moment, naked before her; and, finally, as he visibly forced himself to leave.

Cassie turned thoughtfully to her typewriter. With the echo of their laughter still lingering in the room and her feelings stirred so deeply, she had the most productive session with her novel that she had ever experienced. Out of the depths of her own emotions, her characters came alive on the written page.

Spring finally arrived in all its glory as Cassie put the finishing touches on her manuscript and prepared to come to terms with the direction her life was to take.

There were still many unanswered questions. She knew that her career as an editor would be over if she didn't return soon. But could she work with Tony again? Was it possible for them to retain a purely professional relationship? Perhaps her assistant had done such a good job that she was no longer needed.

Then there was her novel. Was it as good as she thought it was? Would Hamilton House publish it? It was a departure from their normal fare and not the one they thought she was writing. It was an historical novel, an inspiring love story, one which would leave the reader with a feeling of hope. Yes, she knew it was good; and they would publish it, if only Tony didn't become vindictive.

And David—what was this strong attraction she felt toward him? And how did David feel? Last week after their ride, she had seen something in his eyes that had sent a thrill to her innermost being. Yet the look had been so brief, so elusive, she told herself that she was mistaken. After all, he hadn't been back since.

These questions ran rampant through her mind as she drifted off to sleep.

The telephone's sharp ring pierced the morning air and jerked Cassie from the half-sleep that claimed her. The clock said 8:04.

"Hello?" she drawled sleepily into the phone.

"Ms. Cassandra Delaney, editor of *Woman's Life* and famous journalist, this is the eminent country doctor, David McBride, calling to invite you on a journey into yesteryear. By truck and by foot, I propose to take you on my rounds today. If my charming company is not enough to entice you, then perhaps the chance to enhance your book might. Either way, I win!"

"Oh, David, I'd love to, but I have to exercise Shebazzi today," Cassie responded, her disappointment apparent.

"Fine. My place is two miles from you if you use the old Wacomaw Trail. Just ride over here and that will be enough exercise for you both. Doctor's orders," he concluded.

"That makes sense. When shall I be there?"

"I need to leave around ten in order to be back by four."

"Oh? Some exotic date with a beautiful creature, no doubt," Cassie teased.

"As a matter of fact, I'm expecting some 'out-land furriner,'" he continued the bantering. "I have an appointment with one of my dad's business associates. Strictly business, I assure you."

"Sounds intriguing. I think I'll stick around to meet him," Cassie decided.

"That's fine with me, but I don't think you'd find the details too interesting," David replied after a slight pause.

Cassie's journalistic ear noted the hesitation. "Does your dad still want you to come home?"

"Uh, yes. How did you know that?" he queried.

"I pieced it together from the bits and pieces you and Pop told me last fall right after Pop's accident. Ever since then, you've been a closed book about your past. Any particular reason?" Cassie asked seriously.

"Ma'am, I thought maybe a 'man of mystery' might be more appealing to you, but, since you asked, I'd really like to tell you all—the whole David McBride epic. 'Course it will take several hours, so let's postpone it until I see you—in about two hours?"

Cassie laughingly agreed. "Right, see you then."

Cassie bounded out of bed with enthusiasm and into the lovely old bathroom paneled with beaded pine and stained a rich red-gold. She turned the porcelain knobs on the oversized, claw-footed bath tub. Soon steam was rising from the tub as the jet of water turned warm. Cassie poured a touch of fragrance from a vial sitting on the tub and paused briefly to enjoy the aroma.

There was precious little of the perfumed bath oil left. It had been mixed especially for her. The scent was hers alone, her trademark.

It had been an expensive gesture on Tony's part, one of those thoughtful extravagances he had used to woo her. They had been on a business trip to Paris and his attentiveness had been increasingly more difficult to ignore.

Paris had been beautiful that spring—and the trip had turned into more pleasure than business. It was her first visit to the City of Lights and what better guide was there than Tony Hamilton Saikas, thoughtful, considerate, and as undemanding as a nineteenth-century suitor.

They had had a wonderful time. Tony had been there before, and he knew all the right places to take her. They walked along the Seine in the dazzling sunlight and visited the Louvre to admire its treasures. Tony bought her flowers from the markets on the Ile de la Cité, and they strolled hand in hand under the Arc de Triomphe and up the Champs-Elysées. They viewed the Eiffel Tower's lacy ironwork from the Palace of Chaillot gardens. In the evening they watched the twinkling lights of the city below from the heights of Montmartre. One day they left in early afternoon and drove to the country to dine at a century-old inn.

On their last day in Paris, Cassie remembered, Tony had taken her shopping. They had gone to Angelique's, the new designer who had taken the Paris shows by storm, and had ordered Cassie a whole new wardrobe, including the perfumes.

He had smothered her protests with assurances that the magazine was buying them. He said she needed them purely from a business standpoint. As editor of *Woman's Life*, she had a certain image he wanted her to portray, and even her salary could not afford what he felt she needed.

That night, Cassie dressed in one of her new evening gowns. As she appraised her appearance, she knew that nothing she had ever accented her dark beauty as this did. The look in Tony's eyes confirmed her appraisal.

Cassie was descending the ornate staircase in the hotel lobby when Tony walked in. He came to an abrupt halt as he slowly took in her beauty. From the lovely, upswept dark curls and large eyes luminous with excitement, his eyes moved to her slender neck, adorned with a single strand of lustrous pearls, to her gown of deep violet whose soft fabric accented her small waist and draped provocatively over small, well-rounded hips. Whatever her misgivings had been about the rest of her new wardrobe, she knew that that gown was worth its price. The vivid color was so right for her, the fit so perfect, the fabric so fine. She knew she was beautiful, and she enjoyed the sensation.

That night, her resistance finally broke. She did not know whether it was Tony's chaste persistence or the timing. When Tony left her at her door that evening, he kissed her gently and she responded with a warmth and passion that surprised them both.

Cassie shook her head as if to clear it of the painful memories—of warm kisses shared that she thought were love, but for him were only—well? What?

Desire? Yes. Lust? Some of that, too. Mostly, she thought in retrospect, it must have been a challenged vanity. She knew that no other woman had been able to resist the charms of Tony Saikas. She saw the admiring glances of women everywhere when he walked into a room. His reputation for breaking hearts was one of the reasons she had resisted his attention, yet he had convinced her that he loved her.

Cassie smiled a bitter little smile and silently mused, *How could someone so wise in some areas be so foolish in others? Why? Did I fool myself? Was I really in love with Tony or could it have been his wealth and his position? Did I really want him?*

Leaving the questions unanswered, Cassie turned quickly and stepped into the tub. She let the comforting warmth of the fragrant water envelop her and wash away the unpleasant questions.

"Whatever it was, it's over, so where do I go from here?"

With that, she finally had verbalized the painful question that had been clamoring in her subconscious for the past months.

Chapter Seven

Cantering Shebazzi through the woods, Cassie felt strangely tranquil despite her painful soul-searching earlier.

The warm bath and brisk ride had eased her tension and, if she were honest with herself, she would have to admit that the excitement of spending the day with David made it easier to dismiss painful memories and to delay uneasy decisions.

Cassie was curious about the doctor's place. She'd never been there—never been invited, in fact. Aubry had said it was a nice country house, but she didn't know exactly what he meant by that description. She supposed it was a small log cabin in keeping with a country doctor's income.

Just then, the horse and rider rounded another sharp turn, and Cassie gasped as she saw a large two-story house of cedar perched on the side of a tall hill. A broad porch ran across the front, and Cassie instinctively knew that it must have a breathtaking view of Falls Fast Creek and the valley below.

Once again the country doctor had surprised her. A small log cabin it wasn't, yet it blended so well into its surrounding that it appeared more like a lodge or retreat. Cassie liked it and was eager to see inside as she rode into the yard.

David hailed her as he came out the back door.

"Right on time, cowgirl. Do you think Shebazzi got enough exercise?" he teased.

"Shebazzi and Cassie, too. You didn't tell me that I was going on a mountain trail ride," the girl replied as she dismounted.

"You ain't seen nothing yet, gal. Just wait until we go on my call this afternoon. That's why I bought this rover."

"David, your place is beautiful. I'll bet there's a good view from your front porch."

"Come in and see for yourself. What's that?" he asked as he noticed her take a bag from Shebazzi's saddle.

"I've got a change of clothes. These jeans are muddy. Could I borrow a room to change in?" she inquired.

"Sure. Come on in. I'll put Shebazzi in the barn while you change," the doctor replied as he opened French doors and admitted Cassie into a large, open room with a massive stone fireplace on the far end. An oversized sofa covered in soft, earth-toned fabric faced it, and two large lounge chairs were on each side. Chairs and tables were placed in intimate groupings around the room. A large grand piano dominated the opposite corner near a window which looked out on the valley below.

The room's massive size, accentuated by tall ceilings, overwhelmed Cassie for a moment, but she soon felt the inviting atmosphere of the warm colors and fine antique pieces. "Such a large room; in fact, such a large house for one person," she commented.

"I know. The original owner built it for a hunting lodge, so I just left this room large. I've remodeled the rest of the house to suit my current needs," he explained as he steered her to double doors leading out of the room into a wide center hall. She noticed braided rugs on the wooden floors; rich, cheery paneling; and fabric wall coverings of subdued but warm colors. As the couple entered the hall, a grandfather clock, its large brass pendulum swinging back and forth, chimed the quarter hour.

David showed Cassie up the slightly curving stairway to his suite, saying, "This is really where I live. Except when I have guests or eat I do most of my living up here. So welcome to my den."

He didn't need to tell her. She would have known that this bedroom was his. It was amazing that the inanimate can be so permeated with the essence and personality of a person. It was clean and neat. The furnishings were totally masculine. There was a massive cherry bed in the center of the room, one that would accommodate his large frame. A much-used leather chair and a small table were placed near a window that reached from floor to ceiling with a commanding view of the valley.

Cassie shivered at the intimacy of the moment. Here she was standing beside this gentle giant. His nearness always disturbed her. She was in his room. The things he loved were here. He dreamed, worked, and lived in these rooms; and they seemed as warm and vibrantly alive as he.

Even now, there was a tray with the remnants of toast and coffee sitting on it. The morning paper from Louisville and a brown leather Bible lay beside the tray.

"My breakfast," he explained. "Mrs. Sloan has come to clean today, so I just left it where I finished it."

"Mrs. Sloan?" Cassie questioned.

"Yes, her husband was one of my patients. After he died, she needed a job, so, twice a week, she rides down with her son Paul and cleans the house. Paul picks her up on his way home after work. He's one of the few young men to get a job down in the valley. She's very proud of him, and so am I," David concluded.

"Your devotion to these people never ceases to amaze me," Cassie commented as she strolled over to the open door opposite his bed. "The sacrifices you've obviously made in order to stay here never seem to bother you. I still find that hard to understand."

"I really don't see that I am sacrificing anything; it seems more like an exchange. I've found a fulfillment here working with them that I never knew was possible," was his quiet explanation.

A wistful Cassie turned and entered the other room. Her eyes fell on a striking portrait of a stately lady.

"David, who is this beautiful woman?" Cassie exclaimed.

"I'm glad you like it," David replied as he came to stand close behind her. He put both hands lightly on her shoulders. "That is a portrait of my mother, done right after she married my father. Most of the downstairs furnishings, at least the antiques and piano, were hers. She would have been a concert pianist, but she gave it up for love."

Cassie moved away from David's disturbing presence and looked at the portrait. Given a few moments, she would have known it was his mother. She saw the same gentle blue eyes staring out from a face of perfect proportions. A slight smile curved the rose-tinged lips; spun-gold curls cascaded to the young woman's shoulders, creating a perfect frame for her soft, feminine loveliness. The artist had captured a serene radiance in her beauty.

The countenance puzzled Cassie, especially in the light of what David had just said, so she asked, "Why did she have to give it up?"

"My dad felt that a wife and mother should stay at home and be just that," he replied with a simple acceptance that irritated Cassie.

"A selfish attitude! Didn't your mother resent him for depriving her of a life of her own?" Cassie asked heatedly.

"No, as a matter of fact, she didn't. She told me that life was a series of choices, and our responsibility was to decide what our purpose is on this earth, to make those choices accordingly, and never to look back with regret. To my knowledge, that's what she did. Her faith and encouragement is one of the reasons I'm here in this place now."

"Oh? Your mother encouraged you to come here? I thought your dad wanted you home?"

"No, my mother never saw this place. She died before I came here. But she had told me God had a special plan for my life and that, in order for me to be happy, I would have to find that purpose. At first, I ignored her counsel because I was determined to make a place for myself, meaning wealth and position," David explained with a wry grin. "I really thought my dad had the right idea where God was concerned. He paid his dues on Sunday, went to church regularly, but he dedicated his life to the pursuit of fame and fortune, which he achieved in great measure," David continued.

As his mood grew pensive, he added, "Dad was a struggling young doctor when he met my mother. He was so captivated by her quiet beauty that he fell deeply in love with her. She was the only child of a wealthy St. Louis family, but Dad would never use her money. I think he always felt that he had to prove himself—but not for Mother's sake. She adored and encouraged him."

"What about their religious differences? Didn't that cause conflict between them?"

David smiled slightly, remembering, and answered, "You'd think so, but, as far as I know, there were none. Mother loved him and gave him her support. She never complained when he worked long hours and was gone from home for days and weeks setting up his clinics. He owns a chain of clinics that caters to the wealthy. Places you can go to get the fat trimmed and the sags lifted. It proved to be a very lucrative venture."

Cassie noted the sardonic note in David's voice. "How about you, doctor? You seem a little bitter."

"Bitter? Maybe so, but I hope not. But, hey, we're getting into the David McBride epic, and I was saving that until later. You get dressed and come on downstairs. I'll be waiting." David abruptly ended the conversation and the brief cloud of sadness and bitterness seemed to vanish.

Alone in the room, Cassie studied the portrait of the blond young beauty whose gentle eyes seemed to reflect an inner peace that Cassie found so mysteriously elusive.

How wonderful it would be to know life was headed in the right direction, she thought to herself.

Cassie reached into her bag and pulled out her pale yellow slacks and sweater. Her face reflected disappointment that the small bag and long ride had left them crumpled. She briskly shook the clothes out, but the wrinkles seemed etched in the soft wool.

"Well, I guess it'll be muddy jeans after all," she said aloud, as she took her brush and lipstick out of the bag.

Crossing over to David's massive bureau, she stood on tiptoe to peer into the mirror, but when she could only see the top of her head, she went in search of another one.

Opening a door across from his study, she walked into a large dressing room with a full-length mirror covering one wall and a robe casually draped over a chair. She knew from the monogram that it was David's—and impulsively she picked it up and tried it on!

She chuckled when she saw her reflection in the mirror. The sleeves fell well below her hands and the hem reached her ankles. All remnants of her former depression lifted as she rubbed her face against the soft maroon fabric and smelled the masculine aroma of David's aftershave. Once again she noted the strange way David's personality permeated his belongings, and she felt as if his inner strength had enfolded her with warmth and security.

Reluctantly she took off the robe and hung it on the brass coat rack attached to the bathroom door. Returning to the mirror, she brushed her hair and touched her lips lightly with soft coral lip gloss.

She took one last look in the mirror and flicked off

the light, leaving the room with her good spirits restored in the anticipation of spending an entire day with David.

"Well, lovely lady, you look refreshed and ready. I like that blue sweater—my favorite color, you know," he commented as he gave her an appreciative glance and smile. "Mrs. Sloan has fixed us a picnic lunch, and I know just the place to enjoy it. It'll be quite a climb through the woods, but worth it. Sometimes I go there just to think and sometimes to fish a little," he said with a twinkle in his eye and his mouth set in the now-familiar crooked grin.

"I can't wait to get started," Cassie responded.

"I've one call to make today, if you don't mind. The roads are rough, especially after that rain Sunday night, but I don't think we'll have any trouble getting back in time for my appointment. Let's be on our way." He retrieved a large wicker hamper from the counter as they passed through the kitchen. "Our lunch," he proclaimed.

The drive down to the road from the house was breathtaking. The trees had tender buds on them. Now and then a dogwood blossom peeked out of its green envelope. The maple trees were resplendently dressed in delicate red blooms. Nature's rebirth was taking place with the backdrop of a cloudless azure sky.

The narrow driveway followed Falls Fast Creek for a quarter of a mile and then crossed the creek on a rustic wooden bridge just before turning onto the road.

"This was once an old logging road and the bridge was built years ago. Many creeks don't have bridges—you just have to ford them—but this creek's deep here. Occasionally, in the summer, I swim near the bridge; the water is so cold it's an exhilarating experience," he said as the rover clumped across loudly.

David laughed at Cassie's alarmed expression. "It's safe. I had an engineer check it last fall."

Soon they were on the main road, and Cassie relaxed as she looked appreciatively at the wide lanes and sufficient shoulders bordering the ravines on the side of the road.

Soon the comfort of the paved road was exchanged once more for the uneven ride of the gravel path and they began to wind around a serpentine trail that would accommodate only a vehicle like David's. With each passing mile, Cassie saw the wisdom in the doctor's decision to invest in the landrover.

They continued on the rough road for three or four miles, until David pulled over to the side of a level indention in the hill and pointed to a slight drop-off.

"We have to walk down that bank. You can't see it from here, but down beneath the road and around that bend is a cabin. Do you remember the twin boys that I delivered last fall? That's where they live. I need to give them their last round of shots," he explained.

The trail down to the house was not as steep as it had appeared from the road and it took the two of them less than five minutes to arrive at the cabin below.

Cassie marveled at the difference in the appearance between this house and the other ones that she had visited with David. This was also a two-room shanty furnished sparsely, but sparkling clean. The gray board floors had been scrubbed almost white and the windows shone.

Jenny welcomed them in, and soon David was about his business tending his patients. They were plump, gurgling cherubs who laughed with delight when David took them on his knee.

Unbidden thoughts of what a fine father David would make drifted into Cassie's mind as she observed his gentleness and honest affection with them.

Young Jenny's eyes were full of admiration for the doctor. She told Cassie, "If it weren't for Doc, I wouldn't have my babies, and Jerry wouldn't have me. Doc Dave stayed with me and wouldn't leave 'til he knew I'd be all right. I named one baby David and the other Jerry after my man."

The visit lasted only a few minutes and soon David

and Cassie were making their way back to the rover. Both were quiet, as if in their own world of thought.

David broke the mood when they were back in the rover by informing her, "There is one more stop I'd like to make, if you can take these rough roads."

"I can take it. You just drive!" she laughed at him. "Another patient? One I've met before?"

"No, not this time. There's a delightful lady who churns delicious butter, and I want some for our bread. Her name is Mrs. Jones. After that I'm all yours until four, you lucky lady. It's all clear for picnic time. Suit you?" he teased.

"Suits me. I am getting a little hungry; and as for your exclusive company, I do think that might be kind of nice; that is, if you've got a really good picnic lunch in that basket!" she laughed.

They continued down the winding road for another few miles in pleasant conversation until David stopped at a house similar in style to other houses in the area. However, it was near the road and the yard was scrupulously clean, with no hint of abandoned cars, stray parts, or old tires.

A slight, gray-haired woman about five feet tall came to the door. She was dressed in a clean, starched calico dress that reached to her black high-top shoes. Her blue eyes twinkled with merriment and her delight in seeing David was genuine.

"Hello, Grandma Jones. Do you have some butter?" David called. "Like you to meet Cassandra Delaney."

"Shore do, Doc. Come on. You must be Pop's Cassie," she responded with a warm appraisal. "The butter's down in the springhouse, Doc, and I've got some blackberry jam for ya. I put it up last summer but I keep forgettin' to give it to you."

Cassie stood quietly looking from one to the other as the warm conversation bobbed about her. Finally, her attention was drawn exclusively to David, as he asked the old woman about her eight children, calling each of them by name! Once again she marveled at the depth of his concern.

"Cassie, you wait here while I run down to the springhouse to get the butter," David said, slipping out the door and leaving her alone with the pert mountain lady.

"Come on in here, missy, while I get his jam," Grandma Jones invited as she went into a large kitchen with a big cast iron stove presiding over one corner. "How long ya been in love with David, girl?" she asked the startled Cassie.

"Beg your pardon?" Cassie stammered.

"How long ya been in love with the doc?"

"We're just good friends. I've only known him a little over six months," Cassie offered lamely.

"Don't ya go tellin' me that, girl. I know that look. Ya look like ya got a fire glowing inside ya ever time ya look at him and for knowing him just six months—well—when I laid my eyes on my Jeff, I knowd he's the one, and that fire inside me never went out for the fifty years we lived together. His love warmed me through the cold nights and made me want to get up in the mornings. I never lived with him so long that my heart didn't skip a beat when he come in at night, and I stood on tiptoe a-lookin' up at him and he called me his 'Marney.' It's been lonely without him but my memories keep me goin'. Yea, ya love him. I can see't in yore eyes. Yur a lucky woman: he's a man for lovin'. Well here 'tis, here's the jam," she declared, ending her observations just as David reappeared.

He didn't seem to notice Cassie's flushed face, as she fought to control some undefined emotion threatening to engulf her.

"Thanks, Granny. You're a love," David said, giving the older woman a hug. "Come on, Cassie, I'm hungry as a bear!"

Taking Cassie's hand, he pulled her rapidly out of the house and down the steps. As she ran to keep up, he lifted his hand in farewell to Grandma Jones.

Chapter Eight

"We're almost there. See that ridge? It's just on the other side, but we'll have to park here," David explained as they left the road some five miles from Grandma Jones' cabin.

"We have to climb up there?" Cassie questioned with a doubtful tone.

"Yes, but it's worth it. Seems like you can see all of Kentucky from that point—and there's a waterfall. You'll see! We're not more than three miles from your place as the crow flies. If we'd taken the horses and gone north on the Wacomaw Trail, eventually it would have ended here. I'm surprised you've never ridden this way," David chattered enthusiastically.

Cassie thought David looked younger than his thirty-five years as he exuded boyish enthusiasm. "Well, let's go. I like a good hike," she answered.

The couple entered the woods and, for a few minutes, the only sounds disturbing the quietness of the moment were their soft footsteps on the straw-carpeted forest floor.

Cassie remained mute as she savored the moment and the place. The evergreen trees towered above her, their large branches forming a verdant canopy which filtered the sunlight. Here and there a small clump of violets sprang up, touches of purple searching for elusive sunbeams.

Still the couple didn't speak. Their silence was one of shared reverence. Cassie felt as if she were in a huge cathedral—and, as she had at Christmas, she experienced an acute awareness of God. A yearning for the faith of her childhood tugged at her heart; yet she resisted, even as she longed for the tranquility of the moment to be made permanent within her.

The trail made a sharp turn and, shortly ahead of them, they could see bright sunlight where the forest ended and the climb began. The trail narrowed, forcing them to walk in single file. They paused for a moment, shielding their eyes from the dazzling light. David pointed upward, and Cassie spied a rock-strewn trail winding around the mountain. There were some trees on the hillside, but the dense forest was behind them.

David answered Cassie's questioning look. "No, we don't go to the very top of the mountain; only about three-fourths of the way up. Let's start climbing."

Twenty minutes later, the two were breathing heavily and had traversed the steep trail with Cassie leading the way. David walked behind her with the heavy hamper.

When they rounded the last corner, Cassie gasped in surprise. She saw a large plateau carved in the side of the mountain. The edge of it was a sheer drop of more than one hundred feet with a broad vista of the valley below. The sky was a brilliant blue, with the distant mountain sides and hollows curtained by a smoky haze so typical of the Appalachian Mountains.

A sprightly stream cascaded down from above and ended in a sparkling clear pool on Cassie's left. A shift in the soft breeze greeted them with a kiss of fine mist from the falls.

"What a lovely place. No wonder you wanted to come here!" Cassie exclaimed when she caught her breath. "Do you come here often?"

David smiled, obviously pleased by her delight, and

79

replied, "As often as I can slip away. I've wrestled with many decisions in this place and somehow I always find the answers I'm looking for."

"How did you discover it, David?" Cassie inquired, still awed by the pristine beauty of the place.

"I own it. Do you remember the old schoolhouse that I told you about? Well, it's up the road from where we left the rover. When I went to look at that place, I learned there was a distress sale on the forty-five acres surrounding the building, so I walked over it. That's when I found this spot—it's part of the acreage."

The doctor continued, "The old-timer who showed me the terrain said that you could see fifty miles from here on a clear day, and I don't believe he exaggerated!" David walked around the pool toward the falls. "Let's spread our lunch right here. I have some gear stored in the cave behind the falls. One afternoon I got caught up here in a torrential rainstorm and had to spend the night. I vowed that I'd leave a change of clothes, blanket, and first aid supplies as well as food and fuel for emergencies. You know the old Boy Scout motto!"

By this time, Cassie had walked past David and was peering cautiously into the cave. "I've never been in a cave before. Is this one very large? What are these for?" she asked as she picked up some books wrapped in plastic and a box of fishing tackle.

"The best thing to have in an emergency! What if I caught fishing fever? Sure would need that; and, if I got stranded, the books could pass the time of day," he chuckled. "Now, come over here and let's eat."

"Well, I'm ready. You didn't tell me how far I'd have to come before I got to eat," she teased.

"Just wanted you to work up a healthy appetite. Trying to put a little meat on those bones," the doctor drawled as they continued the warm banter.

"So, you don't like the way I look. David McBride, you may give me a complex implying that I'm too thin," Cassie pursed her lips in a mock pout. Returning from the cave, she dropped down on the blanket beside him. She stretched her legs out in front of her and leaned back on her hands, peering up into his face.

David stopped unpacking the lunch and gave her a long, lingering appraisal and said seriously, "Cassie, you couldn't look any better to me."

Cassie's face flushed at the compliment, but she held the doctor's eyes in a steady gaze as she responded, "Well that's a relief. Your approval means a lot to me."

"I approve, I approve!" he said softly with a low chuckle as he placed the last container of food before them.

When Cassie had poured their cups of hot tea from the Thermos, David took her hand, and, bowing his head, prayed aloud. His simple prayer of thanks touched Cassie deeply, here, in this arcadian glade.

He squeezed her hand in warm affection before letting it go. They spread the fresh bread with the butter and jam Grandma Jones had given them and ate hungrily from a bountiful feast of fried chicken, baked beans, and potato salad.

The meal vanished rapidly as they gave their full attention to the delicious food. Soon the only thing remaining was the dessert of apple tarts, which they decided to save for a mid-afternoon snack.

"Well, Dr. McBride, you're right. Mrs. Sloan is a marvelous cook. I've never eaten anything better in a New York restaurant."

"Thank you, ma'am, I aim to please. If you'd stick around these hills, you might find a whole lifestyle better than that in New York," he observed with a light tone as he stretched out his long body and propped his head on his hands.

Cassie studied him for a moment. His words were playful, but she sensed a serious intent. Before she could determine his meaning, he asked, "Cassie my love, what would you like to do now? We can't go swimming; it's a little cool for that. So would you like to go sightseeing? We could explore the cave or climb to the top of the falls."

"That's a hard decision; I'm filled to the brim and too lazy to move. Could we just sit here for a while and talk?" Cassie suggested. Turning to face David, she became acutely aware of his nearness.

David sat up slowly and, putting his face very close to hers, said, "I really don't know how safe you'll be if you look at me like that one more time."

Cassie's brow wrinkled as she tried, once again, to determine if he were teasing. His voice sounded serious, but his eyes were twinkling. "Oh, you say that to all the girls you bring up here, Doctor," Cassie lightly responded.

"I've never brought another woman here, Cassie. This place is too special," he murmured.

Cassie acted as if she hadn't heard the last remark. Her heart was pounding at the implication in it, and joy filled her being. "Well, maybe I would like to explore the cave, after all," she mused. With that, David jumped to his feet and reached down to help her.

He took her hand and forcefully pulled her up, but one of her feet caught in a fold of the blanket; and, as he reached out to steady her, his arms went around her. Suddenly, Cassie was engulfed in his embrace. He crushed her to him, and she lifted her face to receive his kiss.

Her hands were on his shoulders and she felt the rough texture of his jacket. The masculine fragrance of his aftershave teased her senses as she felt his lips cover hers. Her warm response unleashed a fire in him that threatened to overwhelm them both.

The kiss was long and deep. Cassie relished the strength of David's arms about her. As his lips pressed hard against hers, every fiber of her being responded to the message David was giving her with his kiss, with his embrace. She could feel the pounding of his heart and knew that his kiss was one of love as well as desire, and her heart filled with happiness in the knowledge.

David did not release her when he raised his lips from hers. He murmured, "Do you know how long I've wanted to do that, Cassandra Delaney?"

She shook her head and smiled up into his face.

"Since that first day I talked to you in your kitchen. I've tried to resist you, but, I love you, Cassie. I want you with me always. Will you marry me?" he asked, his eyes burning with intensity.

"Oh, David, I…I don't know. We've got to think—to talk," she stammered as she tried to pull away from him.

David's arms held her firmly and wouldn't give way to her squirming, "Cassie, your lips just told me what your voice denies. What's wrong?"

"It's just that I'm so confused, David. I thought someone loved me once before, and I was hurt because I listened and believed. I promised myself that I would never be in that position again," she said quietly as she dropped her head, refusing to meet his eyes.

Putting his hand under her chin, David lifted her face to his. He bent his head and kissed her forehead very gently. Then he moved his lips to her eyes, which were now closed, to her cheek, then very softly to her up-turned lips. He kissed her gently, ever so gently, but his kisses were replete with love. "Cassie, I want to take care of you and protect you from hurt. Let me do that," he murmured against her hair.

The tension left Cassie's body as the safe haven of David's arms seemed to shut out the turmoil and hurt of the past months. "Oh, David, I want to love you, but how can I marry you? We live in different worlds and I don't know if I can live in yours. What about my career? How could a marriage survive with me in New York and you here?" she wondered aloud.

David dropped his arms from around her and, taking her by the hand, led her to the base of a nearby tree. He sat down and pulled her down beside him. As soon as she was seated, he put his arm around her and pulled her close. "That's a good question, Cassie. What *about* your career? I've sensed that things are unsettled for you back at *Woman's Life*. This leave of absence seems more than just an interlude to write your book. Want to tell me about it?"

With a deep breath that came as a half sob, Cassie began her story. "There is a man back in New York—one whom I thought I loved. He said that he loved me, but what he called love was not enough for me. He wanted a relationship without commitment. He's my boss, the publisher of *Woman's Life*, Tony Saikas.

"I took a leave of absence so I could sort out my life, and my time's about up. I've thought a great deal about Tony and now I wonder if I ever really loved him. His lifestyle was exciting and his attention flattering, but I think now that I probably didn't love him. Oh, David, suppose I just don't know how to love *anyone*!"

"I'm not worried about that, Cassie. I know that you love me, whether or not you know it. Now tell me about your job," David probed.

"Well, that's another problem. I don't know if I even have a job now, but a career is very important to me. So are money and position. David, I don't think I could be happy back in these hills trying to make do on a small income. How would you feel if I lived in New York and you lived here, or maybe you could move to New York," she said weakly.

"No, Cassie. I guess I'm like my father in some respects. I want my wife to live here with me. I would be proud to have you continue your career—as long as you could do it here. As for my moving, I can't. Well, I said that I'd tell you the story of David McBride today. It's not a very long or pretty story. It's just one about a young man who thought that position and money could bring the ultimate happiness. They didn't.

"When I was in college, I drove the smartest car, dated the most beautiful girls, and had my heart set on attending a good medical school. I lived life in the proverbial fast lane and fooled myself that I was living it to the fullest. One morning, I woke up and realized that I was empty and unhappy. I had just been turned down by the medical school I wanted to attend. That got my attention, because I really wanted to be a doctor. I thought I wanted it for prestige and position, but, when it looked as if I couldn't get into medical school, I came face to face with life's issues. My mother's counsel came back loud and clear: no matter what you do or who you are, if you do it because God wants you to, then you are successful and fulfilled. I faced up to life and made some choices. I buckled down to studying and finally I was accepted into medical school. It was hard but wonderful to have a purpose—to be the man and the doctor that God wanted me to be. I was so content until you came into my life, Cassie. Now, I have a deep yearning for you, but God has called me to work here and my wife will have to share that calling." David finished his story with a tender smile.

"Oh, David, can't we discuss this without bringing God into it? Can't we decide what's best for us on our own? I don't even know what you mean by God's 'calling' you to work here. How could I share your life with you when I don't understand what you're talking about? I believe in God; I know that Jesus Christ is His Son, and that He died so I could be forgiven for my sins and go to heaven when I die. But I'm not convinced He's interested in what I do with my life *here and now*," she cried, in a torrent of emotion.

"Cassie, whatever gave you an idea like that? When did you decide that God didn't care what you did?" he asked, perplexed.

"After the death of my parents, I was nineteen years old and all alone. I decided that if I was going to make it in this world, it would be on my own effort, and, David, I've made it—*on my own*. I don't know if I can give all that up—even for you." Her voice trailed off.

The doctor sat quietly, looking down at the beautiful

face, and the dark eyes storming with emotion. Finally, he answered in a whisper, "But, are you happy, Cassie, are you happy?"

The truth of the question seared Cassie and the defiance drained from her visibly. She dropped her head on David's shoulder, fighting desperately against reaching out to him. She wanted to accept his proposal, his terms, and to share his life; yet something, maybe her will, her ambition, or fear, kept her from yielding to his love and to her own, challenged heart.

David gathered Cassie into his arms once more and said softly into her hair, "Darling, I know you're a little fighter. I admire your drive and your determination. It's part of what makes you *you*. We're going to make it, together, you'll see. I won't give you up. I don't know how yet, but I *know* that everything is going to work out for us. God meant you for me, Cassie. Someday, you'll share my life here in these hills and find a joy and fulfillment you never knew were possible." He chuckled as he added, "I've got a lot of love to give you, Cassie, and so has our Lord."

Abruptly changing the mood, he stood up and looked at his watch. "Isn't it a pity? Man's days are ruled by his appointments—and I have one at 5:00. We'd better get started back."

Somehow, David's words of hope calmed the storm that had besieged Cassie. She stood up, feeling that perhaps the answers she sought were very close. A shy smile replaced her tears. As she stood on tiptoe and kissed the tall man's cheek lightly, she remarked, "Any woman would be blessed to be loved by you, David."

Chapter Nine

Cassie stretched her arms skyward as she stepped away from the horse's side for a moment of rest. The tightness in her shoulders relaxed a little as she lowered her arms and touched her toes while bouncing easily from the waist.

"Mmmm, that feels good," she declared as she straightened and resumed her work. It was mid-afternoon and she had been working with the horses since early morning. She had cleaned their hooves, mucked their stalls, and now she was giving Nadia a much-needed rubdown. Reaching for the curry comb, Cassie began to brush with firm, straight strokes.

"Hey, careful, girl," Cassie teasingly scolded, as Nadia flicked a pesky horsefly with her long tail and, at the same time, landed a stinging swat on Cassie's arm.

Cassie brushed the mare energetically to remove the thick, loose hair that had kept the horse warm during the winter. Slowly the first hint of a sleek coat began to show on her neck and flanks.

"A few more days of this, girl, and you'll glisten in the sunlight," Cassie said as she finished currying the horse and patted her fondly on the neck.

The faint roar of a familiar motor caused Cassie to turn expectantly toward the gravel driveway. Hurriedly she untied Nadia and returned her to the paddock just as David's rover came to a stop.

"Hello there, lovely lady," David called as he got out

of the truck. With a few quick strides he stood facing her. For a moment those were the only words spoken as they stood and silently beheld each other. Finally, David tenderly brushed Cassie's cheek with his hand and said softly, "I love you, Cassie. I love you."

A warm smile crossed Cassie's face before she reached up and gently traced David's lips with her finger. "I know," Cassie said as she waited expectantly for David's kiss. He looked at her longingly before saying, "I've brought you a visitor."

Cassie had been so enamored with David that she had failed to notice his companion in Big Bertha. Taking a step around David, she exclaimed with delight, "Billy! Billy Brown! Oh, David, what a nice surprise."

Arm in arm they walked toward the rover as Billy stepped out to greet them. Gone was the frail, sickly boy of last fall. He was still thin, but the color had returned to his cheeks, and he was straight and tall as he walked toward them, a broad grin on his face.

"Billy, David had promised me he'd bring you for a visit when you were well, and from the looks of you I'd say you're fine," Cassie observed.

"Yes ma'am, I feel fit as a fiddle, but Doc's taking me to the hospital to make some tests just to make shore—I mean *sure*—my heart's really okay," Billy informed her happily. "I asked the Doc if we could stop by for a minute so I could thank you in person for readin' my stories and loanin' me your books. It's meant a whole lot to me," he finished shyly and dropped his eyes to the ground.

"I enjoyed reading your stories, Billy. You really do have talent. Let's go up to the house. We'll have some lemonade and visit in the library."

"Cassie," David interjected. "We'll have to take a raincheck. I need to be back by five for the out-of-town visitor I mentioned yesterday. The plane was grounded in St. Louis because of fog, so we're meeting this afternoon instead. I'm sorry. There's nothing I'd like more than to stay," David explained as he put his arm around her.

"We'll make it another time," Cassie responded as she noticed the faint disappointment on the youth's face.

"I shore hope so," Billy replied as they walked toward Big Bertha.

David's arm was still around Cassie when they reached the rover. Stopping by the cab door, he drew her closer and kissed her lightly on the lips. "I'll be leaving early in the morning to see my patients farther north. I'll see you when I get back. You take care, lil' Cassie," David said as his eyes lingered on her lovingly before he climbed back into the truck.

Cassie's eyes glistened with joy as she simply nodded her head to him and waved good-bye.

Cassie closed the farmhouse's massive front door behind her and leaned her tired, happy body against the old oak frame. The light coming through the leaded glass panes created a soft halo effect on Cassie's tousled hair and gave her an air of angelic beauty.

She continued to relax against the door as thoughts of the last two days filled her mind. She gently touched her shoulders and remembered the warmth of David's large hands when he had rested them on her slender frame.

She did not touch her lips, but walked to the mirror that hung on the foyer wall. Her heart quickened as she looked at her deeply tinted lips and remembered the experiences of the last two days. She had not felt this alive in months and it was all because of David. She had never known anyone like him. He was gentle and kind, to be sure, but it was more than just that. He had a deep inner strength that inaudibly proclaimed him to be a man among men.

Even at their first meeting, she had intuitively known there was something different about him. In the passing weeks, he had confirmed her feelings about him as she observed him with Pop, then with Billy, and especially yesterday, as she had watched his gentleness with Jenny's twins and his genuine affection for old Mrs. Jones. Something in his quiet strength drew people to him. She saw it in the eyes of all those who knew him—to them David McBride was, as Pop had once put it, "Some kind of a man."

Cassie laughed softly as she pictured his crooked grin and thought of his dry sense of humor. Bathed in a sensation of warmth and contentment, she relived his tender kisses and yesterday's quiet time of sharing.

Still caught up in the events of the day, Cassie turned from the hall mirror to sit on the small deacon's bench nearby. Just as she moved, her glance fell on an object lying on the small table beneath the mirror. The joys of the past two days shattered suddenly, and the reality of her indecision hit her with full force. Her hand reached down and picked up the current edition of *Woman's World*. She had received it yesterday along with another letter from Tony, this one telling her of a crisis at the magazine.

The last two days have been a wonderful diversion, but it was foolish of me to think that anything has changed, she silently observed. *I have to make a decision, but I don't know what to do. Do I go back to* Woman's Life? *Could I work with Tony again? What about David?*

Leaving her silent questions unanswered, Cassie walked into the living room and over to the sofa in front of the large, open windows. She sat on the down-filled cushions and hoped that the beautiful view and refreshing breeze would clear her thinking.

"Oh, David," she whispered quietly, "what am I to do?" At the mention of his name, an overwhelming longing swept over her. She wanted to be near him, to be close to him, to have the reassurance of his strong presence.

Suddenly, the knowledge that going to New York would mean she no longer could be near David broke through her consciousness with a forceful agony that pierced her heart like a well-aimed dagger. Tears filled her beautiful brown eyes and spilled over her cheeks. A salty taste touched her tongue as she spoke once again. "David McBride, *I love you*! God help me, I really love you!" She paused as the words she had just uttered registered their possible consequences in her already-divided mind. "But even though I love you, David, I could never share your life—not here. I've fought too hard and worked too long just to give it all up the way your mother did."

The fragrance of the day faded as the hopelessness of her dilemma drove Cassie deeper into despair. Folding her arms, she rested her tousled head on the back of the lovely old sofa.

The sound of a car motor coming up the winding drive jerked Cassandra from her depression.

Quickly wiping her eyes, she peered out the window to view the approaching visitor. She noted the classic lines of a sleek sports car as it stopped directly in front of the house. The car door opened, and, to her surprise, it was not a man who got out, but one of the most strikingly beautiful women Cassandra had ever seen.

Cassie stood discreetly away from the window, but still close enough to appraise the flawlessly dressed woman as she strode assertively up the brick walk. Her pale golden hair glinted in the last rays of the sun, and the vibrant color of elegant silk enhanced her deeply tanned figure. She carried a leather attaché case, monogrammed with the letters P.B.

The door chimes rang throughout the house, heralding the woman's presence. At first Cassie did not move, but continued to stare in contemplation. *I know I don't know her, yet there's something vaguely familiar about that woman*, Cassie thought.

On her way to the door she again saw herself briefly in the foyer mirror. *Hair disheveled, dirty clothes, no makeup, and eyes red from crying…I look just great to meet a stranger*. With a shrug of resignation, Cassie answered the door.

"Good afternoon. May I help you?" Cassie asked stiffly, painfully aware of her own unkempt appearance.

"I hope so," came the deep-timbre reply. "I'm Priscilla Bellwood. Is this David McBride's place or can you tell me how to get there?"

At the mention of David's name, Cassie felt as though her heart had stopped. *What did this woman want with David*? Trying to conceal the anxiety in her voice, Cassie answered evenly, "This is not Dr. McBride's ranch; however, his place does adjoin this one. His driveway is just a half mile off the second dirt road to the right."

"Thank heavens. I don't know when I've been so turned around," Priscilla exclaimed. "My plane was grounded yesterday, and, now that I've made it this far, I'm running late. May I use your phone to call David? I don't want him to worry. Since you're so familiar with his place, would you draw me a map?"

"Certainly," Cassie replied, anxious to find out more about Priscilla and her relationship with David. "Come on in, I'm Cassie Delaney. The phone's just over there—and I'll be glad to draw you a map. It's really very easy to find."

Priscilla picked up the phone to call David. Casually drawing a map, Cassie unashamedly listened as the blonde beauty dialed and reached him.

"David, this is Priscilla," she said in a soft voice. "I'm sorry I'm so late. I know you must be worried, but I made several wrong turns on all your mountain roads and I've ended up at the ranch next to yours...yes, the Delaney place. I'll be with you shortly." Priscilla paused and then laughed softly. "I know. I want to get things resolved too. See you in a few minutes." With that, Priscilla hung up the phone and, face aglow, turned toward Cassie.

During the brief conversation, Cassie had tried to remain objective, but seeing Priscilla's face made nagging doubts pull at her heart.

Priscilla declared, "Oh, it was so good to hear David's voice. It's been a long time since we've talked."

"Oh?" asked Cassie. "So you've known David, I mean Dr. McBride, for a long time? Did you grow up together?"

"Grow up together?" Priscilla repeated. "Yes, we did. In fact, we were engaged until about three years ago. Then he decided to come to this Godforsaken wilderness, and I just couldn't give up my career for this." A trace of bitterness filtered into Priscilla Bellwood's voice as she finished.

"I see," said Cassie. "He does seem to have a passion for this place and these people…" Cassie let her sentence trail off.

Priscilla arched her eyebrows quizzically and asked, "Do you know David well?"

Something about the question irritated Cassie. She answered evasively, "Dr. McBride and I are friends. He comes over to check on my elderly caretaker. Here's your map. I don't think you'll have any problem finding your way from here," Cassie concluded as she handed Priscilla the folded paper.

Priscilla paused before she took the map, and, for a moment, her cool blue eyes stared directly into Cassie's warm brown ones.

"Didn't you say your name was Cassie Delaney a moment ago?" Priscilla queried unexpectedly.

"Why, yes I did," Cassie answered, puzzled.

"Could Cassie be short for Cassandra? Are you Cassandra Delaney, editor of *Woman's Life?*" Priscilla smiled warmly at the look of surprise on Cassie's face.

"Yes, I am. But how did you know that?" Cassie wanted to know.

"Well, it wasn't a wild guess. I thought you looked familiar when we first met, but I couldn't place you. Then you said your name, I saw the copy of *Woman's*

Life, and the rest was a simple deduction," Priscilla explained. "I didn't recognize you at first, because you look so different from the first time we met."

"You look familiar, too, but, I'm sorry, I just can't place you. When did we meet?"

"Two years ago your magazine did a feature article on successful women lawyers. I was one of the lawyers covered in the story. A few weeks after the story ran, someone introduced us at a party at Tony Saikas's home," said Priscilla.

"Of course; now I remember you! You were one of the first female attorneys hired by a leading corporation to represent the company in international corporate cases. That was a good article," Cassie said with genuine pride. She was thankful that, for the moment at least, the conversation had turned away from David and toward safer ground.

"You're right, it was a good series, and the personal publicity didn't hurt, either. Since that story, I've become associated with a well-known law firm in St. Louis. If things continue the way I plan, I should be a partner in five years."

"I'm impressed; do you still deal mostly with corporate law or are you more diversified now?" Cassie asked.

"They wanted me because of my corporate experience, so that's all I do. It's really my forte. It's challenging and complicated; and I love it. I guess you could say it's my life," Priscilla said with genuine enthusiasm.

"I know what you mean," Cassie quietly agreed. "One's job can be so absorbing that there's no room for anything else. It really does become your life," Cassie said, not so much to Priscilla anymore, but to herself.

"Then I take it you feel that way about being editor of *Woman's Life?*" Priscilla asked. "You *are* still with *Woman's Life?*" Priscilla continued, with the probing intensity of one searching for more than a polite answer.

Not wanting to reveal her inner turmoil and indecision, Cassie nodded and answered, "You're right, being editor of *Woman's Life* has been my life…but I know you must be going. It won't be long before dark, and, as I'm sure you've noticed, we haven't any street lights yet," Cassie lightly concluded.

Cassie could tell by the look in the blonde lawyer's eyes that the noncommittal answer had not satisfied her. However, it had accomplished exactly what Cassie had intended. It had veiled her frustrations and brought an end to the visit.

Priscilla Bellwood looked at Cassie with cool reserve, then forced a large smile. "You're right. I must be going. David will be expecting me—and we have so much to catch up on. Thanks for the map." With that, she walked out the front door and down to her car.

Cassie continued to stand in the living room as she heard Priscilla's car pull out of the driveway. She seemed frozen to the worn rug, a captive of nagging doubts and ugly suspicions. She was besieged with thoughts of Priscilla and David together at his house…alone.

Finally, with a forcible act of will, she went about turning on lights as the soft blanket of dusk surrounded the house. Cassie felt totally alone.

She wandered to the kitchen to fix a sandwich, thinking that physical activity would help, but her efforts were in vain. She stared absently at the plate before her and left her food untouched.

At last, in despair and resignation, she placed her face in her slender hands. *God, help me*, she softly sobbed. *God, if You're really there, please help me.*

Cassie Delaney was not the only one to speak God's name as the dusk gave way to darkness and cool night air invaded the hills and hollows of the Appalachians.

Dr. David McBride walked slowly to his front door. The headlights of Priscilla Bellwood's car shone brightly into the front windows of his rustic lodge as she pulled into the driveway.

"Lord, give me wisdom," David softly murmured as he opened the front door and stepped onto the rambling porch to greet the beautiful woman from his past.

Priscilla opened the car door and paused briefly before she lifted her long, shapely legs out of the car and walked eagerly toward David.

David did not move as she approached. He found it hard to believe, but she was even more beautiful, more alluring than she had been three years ago.

As he watched her walk toward him, old memories surfaced, reminding him of their former relationship. David shook his head slightly, as if trying to free his mind of those objectionable visions from the past.

Priscilla came up the steps with an easy sway to her hips, as if to remind David of what was once his. However, her voice and her words did not contain the sensual implication of the movements of her body. She spoke with an open friendliness as one friend would to another.

"David, it's been such a long time. It's good to see you," Priscilla said as she reached up to give him a hug.

David returned her hug easily and responded with his familiar crooked grin. "It *has* been a long time, Priscilla. How have things been with you?" He opened the door and ushered her into the spacious rooms of his home.

Priscilla paused before she answered as her eyes surveyed the large room in which she now was standing. "David, I must admit I'm pleasantly surprised," she commented as she walked slowly toward the warmth of the fire burning brightly in the rock fireplace at the far end of the room. "I didn't expect something this grand! Your home is beautiful—and I see you have your mother's piano. I'm relieved to see how well things are going with you."

David smiled easily at Priscilla and said, "I believe

that was my question. How have things been with you?"

"Oh, you did ask me that," she laughed.

Placing her briefcase on the antique table by the fireplace, she turned her back to the warmth of the flames and looked directly at David, who was seated on the arm of the large, earth-toned sofa.

"David, I think I'm doing quite well. I've been with the Taylor and Jones firm for the last two years—you remember them—anyway, there's a very good possibility that I'll be made a partner within five years," Priscilla announced, the look of pride evident on her face.

"Sounds like you have your life all planned out. You've worked very hard, and it's good to know things are going so well for you," David said with sincerity.

Priscilla looked at his handsome face intently. From the cool expression in her eyes, she had expected more than his good wishes.

David, sensing Priscilla's feelings and wanting to keep things light and safe, began to speak of other things. "Well, I take it you've seen my father recently, since you're here as his legal representative. How's he doing? He has refused to write me for the last six months, since I told him again that I didn't intend to come back and take over his clinics," David said matter-of-factly.

"David, David," Priscilla smiled as she shook her head slightly, her golden hair catching the glint of the firelight. "Once I thought you and your father were so much alike, but you two are totally opposite. I don't know how that ever happened…but, to answer your question, he is about the same—he's working hard as always, but it's really beginning to show on him." She obviously hoped that her words would soften David's stern resolve about returning to the Missouri clinics.

For a moment, David said nothing. Then he stood up and crossed to the beautiful piano. "I could explain what happened, but you still wouldn't understand any more than my father does." His large hand lightly touched the ivory keys, and a few notes broke the heavy silence that filled the room.

A hint of anger flashed in Priscilla's eyes, but she quickly changed her expression.

David looked up in time to see the flicker of indignation fade from Priscilla's face. He sensed that she was controlling her words, and searching for the right time to force the issue about his father. David had known Priscilla for a long time. Thinking as a lawyer, she would wait until the mood was more agreeable before she stated her case.

"Dr. McBride, where do you take a poor famished attorney to get a bite to eat?" she jokingly questioned. "My afternoon driving and the unexpected game of travel hide-and-seek has left me starving. Is there a restaurant close by, or must you go out and shoot a bear?"

A grin broke across David's face. "Well it's like this, ma'am. There ain't no eatin' places close by, so I had my housekeeper, Mrs. Sloan, whip us up a batch of vittles before she went home. If'n you think you can handle pork chops, biskits, and green beans, then I reckon you won't starve."

Priscilla laughed with genuine pleasure as she walked over to David and put her arm through his.

"Kind sir, will you please escort me to this sumptuous feast you have just described? I do believe I may succumb at any moment to the vapors!" She leaned her head in mock weakness on his shoulder as they walked into the large country kitchen.

David made no response to Priscilla's flirtation as he walked her to the table and pulled out a chair. "Here, have a seat while I put the food on the table. Mrs. Sloan has taken care of everything. All I have to do is take the food out of the oven."

Priscilla sat down and looked at him quizzically. "Don't tell me you're no longer a male chauvinist? Serving me dinner...how unlike the David I remember. Does this mean you've also changed your archaic ideas that a woman's place is in the home, and that she follows her husband wherever he goeth?" she asked with a teasing lilt to her voice.

Placing the warm food from the oven on a large tray, David walked to the harvest table and set the dishes carefully on the colorful ceramic trivets decorating the green plaid tablecloth. Completing his task, he sat down across from Priscilla before returning for the tea.

"Ms. Bellwood," David began in a mock tone of scholarly seriousness, "after years of intense study, I have not been able to ascertain what male chauvinism is. I assume, from the tone that is so often associated with those two words, it must be some incurable malady. Furthermore, I really don't know what you mean by 'a woman's place is in the home.' If you mean I would expect my wife to live with me wherever my profession takes me, then my position hasn't changed. I do believe marriage is a lifetime commitment that two people make to live together in a shared unity—sharing love, laughter, sorrows and interests. If a man and a woman can't work their careers out in that framework, then they shouldn't marry. The question, if I remember correctly, was never who would do the dishes and who would take out the trash. If my interpretation is chauvinistic, then so be it." Rising from his chair, David bowed his head slightly, as if to signal that he had finished his grand declaration.

He continued, "And as for serving you dinner, I don't intend to let you off Scot free. This is going to be a working meal. Bring in your briefcase so we can eat while you tell me about my father's new intentions for getting me back into his business. It's already 7:30—and there's a comfortable boarding house about thirty miles from here. I took the liberty of making reservations for you when I realized you were running late—and Mrs. Ketchum likes all her boarders in by 11:00."

Priscilla sat for a moment, trying to digest all the things David had just said. With her frustration apparent, she exclaimed, "David, you're not serious—a boarding house? Really? I thought we'd have a quiet dinner, catch up on old times and then talk business. I'm sure you wouldn't send me out to find this Mrs. Ketchum's place in the dark?" Priscilla ended with a sweet plea in her voice.

He recognized Priscilla's manipulative manner and did not intend to allow it to sway him from his plan to end their meeting as soon as possible. He would feel comfortable only when this lovely creature was once again out of his life.

"Priscilla, I have every intention of seeing that you get to Mrs. Ketchum's safely. You can follow in your car while I lead the way in my rover. Now, if you'll bring the papers, I'll pour the tea," and, without another word, David turned toward the refrigerator.

An exasperated Priscilla went back into the living room and returned with a file. Placing it alongside her plate, she slowly flipped through papers while David sat down. Immediately, he bowed his head and asked a brief blessing on the food they were about to eat. Priscilla watched him with obvious amusement as he finished his prayer and lifted his head.

"My, my, I guess that's supposed to make the food taste better," she said flippantly, as she reached for a nearby dish.

"Not only that, Priscilla, but I've found it makes a lot of things better. Now what are those papers you've brought with you?" he asked quietly as he buttered a large, flaky biscuit.

"To put it bluntly, David, your father is going to disinherit you if you don't sign these papers agreeing to take over controlling interest in his clinics within the next two years. He says he'll give you the capital necessary to build a clinic for these...hill people...and will even find competent people to staff it—but only if you return home and take over his clinics."

David put down his knife and was silent for a long

time. Finally he spoke in a quiet but assured manner. "Priscilla, my father's offer is more than generous." David paused before he continued, "I've thought this through. I have struggled with it, because of the obvious financial advantages I would have to help these people…but, despite all of this, I know I must say no—even if my father disinherits me."

Priscilla stood up angrily as he spoke his last words. "David, you're a fool. I know your mother left you a trust fund, but the bulk of her money went to your father. Your fund will run out, but you can have security if you'll just take your father's offer. He's rich and you can have anything…do anything you want." Priscilla's voice rose in frustration as the practiced control of a courtroom attorney was forgotten.

David looked up at her, and, with an expression close to pity, he said, "I wish you could understand. I already have security—all the security I will ever need."

Priscilla stifled her aggravation and then tried a new approach. "Don't tell me you've fallen under the spell of Cassandra Delaney?"

"Cassie has nothing to do with my decision," he said flatly. "I really think it's best if we leave right away. I don't intend to change my mind, and I have early calls to make in the morning. When you finish eating, we'll leave." With that, he got up from his chair and walked into the living room.

Priscilla did not follow immediately, but, when David finally heard the click of her heels on the pine floors, he reached for her briefcase lying open on the couch.

"David," Priscilla said softly, as she reached the couch and gently touched his arm. "I hope you're not angry with me—I still care for you deeply. I just don't want you to throw your life away."

David could feel the closeness of Priscilla's body as her hand lingered on the curve of his arm. With a smooth but decisive move, he handed her the briefcase and stepped away. "No, Priscilla, I'm not angry with you. My life has taken on a different direction over the years, that's all. Come on, we'd better be going."

An obviously discouraged Priscilla walked toward the front door, only to let out a deep throaty laugh as David opened the door and revealed the impenetrable fog that now engulfed the mountains.

"Well, David," she said, trying to conceal the hint of victory in her voice. "Looks like I'll have to spend the night here after all!"

David looked annoyed as he closed the door and returned to the warm glow of the fire.

"My room is upstairs; you can sleep there. I'll sleep on the couch. If you don't mind, I'd like to call it an early night…I need to leave around six in the morning. Can I get you anything?"

"Well, I do have a small overnight bag in my car—if you could bring that in, I think that's all I'll need."

"I'll be right back," he said, as he walked out the door into the fog-shrouded night.

Not waiting for David to return, Priscilla wandered upstairs, anxious to see the rest of the house, especially David's room.

She had little trouble finding it. She admired the masculine features and the warm male ambiance that permeated every corner of the spacious room. Priscilla stopped abruptly as she spied the clear evidence of a recent female visitor.

She walked quickly to David's open closet and pulled out the yellow cashmere sweater and slacks that hung loosely on a wooden hanger. Carefully examining the sweater, she muttered angrily under her breath as her fingers traced the "C.D." neatly monogrammed on the front.

So you and Cassandra Delaney want me to think you're just friends—but, David, this proves it! There is something going on between the two of you.

She hung the sweater back in the closet and closed the door as she heard David's footsteps on the stairs.

102

"Here you are, Priscilla. I'll see you in the morning." David set the overnight bag inside the door and turned to leave.

Priscilla looked at the retreating back of his broad shoulders as he left the room. Irked, she reached for the overnight bag and walked over to the bed. She unlatched her bag and carefully pulled out a silk gown of the palest blue with a delicate lace bodice and small lace straps. Quickly undressing, she slipped into the gown and stood in front of the full-length mirror that hung inside the closet door.

Priscilla smiled at her reflection. The gown was alluring, the fit vividly accentuated her well-proportioned body, and the pale color enhanced her tan and made her blue eyes even more striking. The effect was devastating. With a final appraisal, she turned and left the bedroom.

David was sitting on the hearth, looking into the vivid flames. He held a mug of coffee in his large hands and from time to time took a small sip of the steaming drink. The room was dark except for the firelight gently lighting it and casting dancing shadows on the walls nearby.

David's thoughts were so filled with Cassie that he did not see Priscilla, with her pale gown moving easily against her body, nor did he hear her bare feet descend the stairs and walk with deliberate purpose in his direction.

He was startled when he heard his name, but was shocked when he stood to find her so close—and dressed in a manner that would tempt any man.

"Priscilla, what are you doing here?"

Priscilla smiled invitingly. "Isn't it obvious? I've missed you. And I think you've missed me and what we had together," she said as she moved closer to him.

David turned away as the memories of past experiences flooded his mind. Weighing his words carefully, he said firmly, "Priscilla, it was wrong then and it's wrong now. Then I didn't know the difference—now I do. I love Cassie Delaney, and I've asked her to marry me. I won't risk my love for her or hurt my relationship with Christ. Cassie might never find out, but God would know, Priscilla. It's not worth it—the price of one moment of passion—it's too high."

"David, honestly," Priscilla said with exasperation. "I thought there was something between you and Cassandra Delaney, but as you say, she need never know…but this Christ bit—that's another thing. You say the name like He's someone real. David, look at me," she pleaded. "Love me…I'm real…and I'm here."

David turned to face her and said with finality, "Don't you understand? I'm not the same David McBride you once knew."

As though he had spoken a challenge, Priscilla moved toward him seductively. "David, you couldn't have changed that much," she said as she started to place her arms around his neck.

David reached up and caught Priscilla's arms. He looked at her beautiful face and the flash of anguish and disbelief in her eyes; then, releasing her arms, he walked toward the front door.

"David," she cried, "what are you doing?"

"Fleeing, Priscilla, fleeing." Without looking back, he was gone.

David's ears did not hear the strong expletives Priscilla screamed after him. Outside, the cool night air engulfed him and offered a needed balm from the scene he had just left.

He was glad he was alone. He was visibly shaken by his encounter with Priscilla. How close he had come to yielding to the uncontrolled fire that so easily can claim a man!

"Thank you, Lord," David said quietly, as he walked toward the fog-cloaked barn. "Oh, God, sometimes to flee is the only escape."

Chapter Ten

Cassie listened to the familiar squeak of the front porch swing. She had been sitting there since before six, watching as dark gave way to dawn.

Has Priscilla been at David's all night? she wondered for the hundredth time. *Does he still love her? Would he want her instead of me if she'd agree to stay? I thought he loved me, but why didn't he call last night?* Over and over these thoughts had tumbled through her mind as she had listened to the clock tick away the minutes and hours when sleep had refused to come.

Finally, in the predawn hours she had slipped on her down jacket, David's Christmas gift to her, and had gone out to the front porch.

The swing still was swaying gently as she heard Pop coming toward the house whistling a familiar tune. He had already begun his daily routine—up early, gather the eggs, and feed the livestock before fixing his morning coffee. His tune stopped abruptly as he spied Cassie sitting quietly in the swing.

"Cassie? Cassie, that you?" he asked as he turned from his path and walked toward the porch. "Girl, what are ya doin' jest sittin' in that swing this time a'day?" he asked her.

Cassie didn't answer but only stared down at the wooden floor as Pop walked up on the porch and pulled a rocking chair near enough to sit down and face her.

"Now, girl, I spoke to ya two times an' ya ain't said a word. What's troublin' ya?"

"Pop," Cassie said weakly, "I'm okay. I just couldn't sleep, that's all. You'd better get on with the feeding. The animals will be waiting."

Pop looked intently at Cassie's face. With a gentle firmness, he declared, "Lil' Cassie, I've known ya since ya wuz no bigger than a feather piller. Now them animals won't starve and them chickens can lay a dozen eggs apiece, but I ain't movin' from this rocker, 'til ya start tellin' yur old Pop the truth. What's hurtin' yur heart so?"

Cassie began to cry softly as the old man reached out and took her hands in his tough, calloused ones. "Tell me about it, girl," Pop urged her.

Amidst tears and jumbled words, Cassie managed to tell Pop of David's proposal, her indecision, and finally, of Priscilla Bellwood.

"Well, girl, let's see if we can cut through some of this stuff that's makin' ya so sad. Do you love Doc Dave?"

Cassie nodded her head. "Pop, I do love him...but I don't think that's enough."

"Well, ya could be right, that just might not be enough." Cassie looked puzzled, and he continued. "There's two kinds of love, girl. There's beginning love...and there's a building love, ya know, 'til death parts ya both. When ya tell a body ya love 'em enough to be theirs forever, then yur willin' to put everthin' on the line, because what yur hankerin' for is to build a lifetime together. Yur wantin' to build something that'll stand strong in the good times and the bad times that'll come. Beginning love won't make it to the finish line— it takes that buildin' love to make a marriage. Honey, I'm feared you got the beginnin' love, and Doc Dave's got the buildin' love."

Cassie shrugged her shoulders heavily and leaned

back in the swing. "I think I see what you mean...but my career and all the effort I've put forth to get where I am still mean something to me. Besides," Cassie muttered despondently, "after last night, the good doctor may have changed his mind altogether."

"Girl, the way ya described that thar Prisibelle and 'cause she and Doc was once an item, I know what's in yur head...but yur wrong. She may be purty enough to turn a man's head, but the doc ain't just any man. He's God-fearing, he's honest, and he shore ain't stupid. Ya just gotta trust him."

Cassie looked into the twinkling blue eyes of the caring man. In spite of her sleepless night and frustrated thoughts, she found herself grinning.

"What's caught yur fancy, girl?" Pop asked as he studied her unexpected smile.

"It's Priscilla, not Prisibelle...and Pop," she said as she reached out and touched the brim of his hat, "how long have you been wearing baseball caps?"

"Ever since ya brung me the first one from yur high school team. I like the way they covered my bald spot and shaded my eyes. They're real handy when I go a-huntin' too."

"Pop, you're something else! You love chocolate bars, cartoons, baseball caps, hard work, and hunting, and," she added tenderly, "you're as wise as Solomon. I love you, Pop. I love you!"

The old man shyly dropped his eyes as Cassie finished. "Ah, girl, quit yur jawin'. I know ya love me."

Cassie looked at him more seriously this time as she bluntly asked, "What am I to do, Pop? What should I do?"

"Well, that question covers a lot of different thangs. About Prisibelle, trust David. About marryin' the doc or goin' back to New York, I can't rightly tell ya what to do, even though I be knowin' what ya oughta do. Lil Cassie, the real problem ain't deciding in whether to choose New York or the doc. The real problem is choosing who's gonna run yur life. Yew decide on that and everthang else'll fall into place."

"You make it sound so simple," Cassie said quietly.

"It is, child, it is. Now I hear Bossy bellowing fer her oats so I best be gettin' on with my chores." Pop slowly got up to leave.

Cassie reached for his hand before he turned to go. "Thanks, Pop. I do feel better. Talking did help. In fact, I think I'll saddle up Nadia and go for a ride. Looks like it's going to be a beautiful day."

"How was your ride?" Pop asked as he walked out of the barn toward the paddock. "Been gone quite a spell."

"It was great, but Nadia and I are both ready to eat," replied Cassie as she swung down from the mare's back.

"Here, Missy, yew go on up to the house and git yur-self somethin' to eat. I'll take care of Nadia," Pop ordered as he took the reins out of her hands.

"Thanks, Pop. I'll come down in a little while and give her a rubdown," Cassie said as she headed toward the house.

Just as Cassie reached the steps, she heard a car pull into the driveway and three staccato beeps of its horn. A wave of panic washed over her as she turned and saw Priscilla Bellwood's car come to an abrupt stop at the end of the walkway.

"Cassandra," Priscilla purred as she got out of the car with her weekender bag over her shoulder. "I'm so glad you're home. I was afraid I might miss you—and David gave me strict orders to stop by and return something to you before I left."

"Oh?" Cassie said evenly as Priscilla walked up the front steps and onto the porch. Cassie hoped that Priscilla would finish her business there on the porch and leave, but the immaculate blonde moved toward the front door. Finally Cassie invited her in.

"I really can't stay long. I have a plane to catch and I need to be on my way. However, David wanted me to make a delivery."

Again Cassie felt the rise of panic as she looked into Priscilla's cold eyes. "A delivery? I'm afraid I don't understand."

Priscilla reached into her weekender and pulled out the yellow sweater and slacks which Cassie had left hanging in David's closet. "David felt, under the circumstances, you'd probably want these back."

Cassie stood silently a moment trying to fathom the meaning of "under the circumstances." Then she reached for the clothes and placed them on the nearby deacon's bench as she carefully responded, "It really wasn't necessary for you to bring them by. I could have gotten them later."

"Well, under the circumstances, David thought it was better if we did it this way," Priscilla said, deliberately emphasizing the "we."

At first Cassie said nothing. Raging within were all the doubts that had tormented her since Priscilla had first rung her doorbell the day before.

In the lengthening silence between the two women, a faint smile touched Priscilla's lips, as if she found pleasure in the stressful quiet.

Finally Cassie broke the spell with one direct question. "Priscilla, you have said 'under the circumstances' twice. Why don't you just tell me what you mean?"

Priscilla smiled smugly. "You know exactly what I mean. I spent the night at David's last night. You know we were engaged once, and our relationship was rather, shall we say, close. He told me he had asked you to marry him…but, after last night, I think you may find things have changed."

The sick feeling in the pit of Cassie's stomach threatened to overwhelm her. She had a strong desire to run from the room, but she looked Priscilla straight in the eyes, forcing herself to respond with a steady voice.

"David has asked me to marry him, but I don't think that your visit with him last night will affect that, one way or the other. He's a God-fearing, honest man." Feeling the strength of Pop's counsel, she declared. "To put it bluntly, Priscilla, I trust David; and I don't believe what you're implying."

The tables had turned, and Priscilla had not expected this firm declaration of trust. Quickly regaining her composure, she smoothly countered, "Cassandra, you can believe whatever you want, but there's a side of David McBride you've never seen. In fact, in many ways he's like your boss, Tony Saikas, only with a softer heart."

At the mention of Tony's name Cassie could feel her stand wavering. "I wasn't aware you knew Tony well enough to compare him with David."

"Oh, I don't really know Tony that well, but I do know his reputation, and, believe me, there are really quite a few similarities between the two. Just as there are *between us*."

Cassie looked at Priscilla coolly. "You and I are nothing alike."

"Now, Cassie—that *is* what David calls you—Cassie? Don't tell me you've told Doctor McBride you'll gladly give up your position at *Woman's Life* to be his little wife and live out your days in these mountains?"

Cassie did not reply, and Priscilla responded victoriously, "I thought not. You want your career, money, and everything that comes with it, more than you could ever want David McBride, even though he is quite a man."

The conversation began to take its toll on Cassie. She did not want to see David in the same light as Tony, nor did she want to think that she could be anything like Priscilla. But there was a ring of truth in Priscilla's last words that she could not ignore.

Gratefully Cassie heard Pop's familiar rap on the back door as he opened it and came in.

"Cassie," he called as he walked through the dining room carrying a basket of eggs. "Oh, there ya are, thought I heard voices in here. Thought you might need some eggs."

At first Cassie was taken aback by Pop's walking casually into the foyer with a basket of eggs. He just stood here, as if both women had been expecting his visit.

"Uh, Pop, this is Priscilla Bellwood, she's, uh…uh," Cassie stammered.

"Oh, I know who she is. She's that city lawyer Doc Dave said was coming to talk about his pa." Pop leveled his twinkling blue eyes at the sophisticated young woman.

"So you're the caretaker Cassandra mentioned yesterday. It seems you know David pretty well, too," Priscilla said.

"Yup, I probably know the doctor better'n most people. In fact, on occasion he's asked me to give him a hand on some thangs—like finding you a place to stay. You enjoy Mrs. Ketchum's boardin' house, or did ya get fogged in last night?"

Priscilla's eyebrows shot up as surprise registered on her face. "I, uh, have never been at Mrs. Ketchum's place. I stayed with David last night," Priscilla replied evenly.

Pop grinned as his wise old eyes looked knowingly at the confident blonde. "Too bad you had to spend the night at the Doc's. Mrs. Ketchum sure does make good biscuits…well, I guess I better put these eggs in the kitchen and get on with my chores…nice meetin' ya," Pop said as he sauntered back to the kitchen.

"David made you a reservation at the boarding house?" Cassie questioned closely.

"So what if he did? That was before I got there and old memories were rekindled. Face it, Cassandra, David is a man. You don't really think he'd tell you what went on last night?"

Cassie walked toward the door. "You've made your

111

delivery and you've said what you wanted to say. Now I think it's time you left," she said as she opened the front door. "And, despite what you say, I do trust David."

Priscilla looked at her briefly before she turned to go. "You sound very convincing, but you'll always wonder if I'm the one David really wants. Anyway it doesn't really matter, because you'll choose your career over him. Bye now."

Cassie fought the urge to slam the door behind Priscilla. *She's right,* she thought to herself. *How can I be sure that it's me David really loves...and how could any man resist Priscilla? Right now I wish I'd never met David McBride. I'm so tired of pain. First Tony and now David. If I could just run away!*

Just then the phone rang. Cassie stood still for a moment, debating whether or not to answer it. Reluctantly she walked toward the phone and picked up the receiver.

"Hello?" Cassie said impatiently.

"Hey, you're already on the defensive and you don't even know who it is! Calm down, my love. This is a business call and that's all," Tony Hamilton Saikas smoothly assured her.

"Your timing has always been uncanny. What's wrong? Hilary has been touching base with me every few weeks, and, the last time I talked to her, she said everything was going along smoothly."

"She would say that. She's been after your job on a permanent basis, so she scrapped some of your plans and implemented her own, hoping to outshine you and ease into your position! She didn't clear anything with me; it was all done under the table. By the time I found out about it, things were in a mess. Hilary did fine as long as she had your detailed plans to go by, but once she deviated, she left us with some real problems."

"Left? Did she quit?"

"I fired her on the spot when I realized what she had

112

done. Cassandra, we need you back...Now!" Tony said emphatically.

"I know it's time for me to come back, but I'm not sure I can work with you again."

"I give you my word that if you come back it'll be strictly business. The magazine needs you, and I'll not put pressure of any sort on you. Can you work under those conditions?"

"I just don't know. Things now are even more complicated than they were when I left."

Slight irritation was beginning to filter into Tony's voice. "Haven't you finished your novel?"

"Yes, I have and it's good, but it's something other than my book."

"Are you going to be more specific, or am I supposed to guess?" an annoyed Tony asked.

"I can't be more specific, I'm sorry. I just feel that I'm at some kind of crossroads, and I don't know which way to turn," Cassie confided with surprise, as she realized how open she was being with Tony.

Tony spoke more patiently, as if hoping to win a favorable decision from Cassie. "I'm sorry you're having a rough time, but you must understand that something you've put your life into for the last three years is in trouble. Cassandra, sometimes you have to put everything personal on hold. The magazine needs you more than ever before. Won't you come back, even if it's only until the magazine is back on its feet?"

David's proposal and now Tony's call had brought the inner turmoil of the past few months to a head. Cassie knew that she must choose as she struggled to give Tony an answer.

"Tony," Cassie began cautiously, "I know you want an answer—but I still need at least a couple of days before I can give you my decision. Please try to understand."

A long silence followed Cassie's request before Tony finally spoke. "Well," he said calmly, "I really don't have much choice, do I? At least it's two days and not six months this time, but you're worth the wait, Ms. Delaney."

Tony's last words alarmed Cassie and she bluntly warned, "You promised it would be strictly business, remember? I'm expecting you to keep your word."

"Hey, I simply meant you're a top-notch editor, nothing more, honest. You have my word, we'll keep it *strictly* business," he concluded amiably.

"All right, Tony, as long as you understand that. I'll be in touch soon, one way or the other," Cassie replied as she ended the conversation.

She returned the receiver to its cradle and slowly walked toward the front window. The sun was now high in the sky, and it was near noon.

How could such a beautiful day contain so many problems? Cassie pondered as she gazed out the window and watched Nadia in the paddock below. *I must decide. But how do I know what to do? What is right for me?*

Nadia pranced about the paddock as if she knew the eyes of her mistress were on her. Once around the fence, twice around the fence she trotted, stopping briefly to toss her proud head toward the farmhouse. Cassie's worried eyes followed each movement of the horse with envy. *How simple things are for you, girl,* Cassie thought. *No decisions; just eat and run fast and free; no responsibilities; no worries.* The more Cassie struggled for the right decision, the deeper she became mired in her own frustrations. Finally, with drooping shoulders and a heavy step, she left the window and headed out the front door to give Nadia her overdue rubdown.

Cassie had just reached the paddock when she heard the familiar roar of the landrover turning off the road and coming toward the barn. Panic gripped Cassie as she realized that soon she would face David. *Not now,* she anguished, *I can't face him now—not after yester-*

114

day and this morning. God, help me—I'm so confused and afraid.

Quickly she left the paddock and took refuge in the barn, hoping that if David did not find her at the house he would think she had gone for a ride or into town.

"How stupid of me," Cassie muttered as the musty smell of feed and hay filled her nose. "Nadia is in the paddock, and my car is parked in the front. If he really wants to find me, he'll come in here to look."

All too soon his handsome physique was framed in the barn doorway. "Cassie, are you in here?" David called as his eyes adjusted to the darker light.

Turning from the doorway and walking over to the feed bin, Cassie didn't answer. Instead she removed the lid from the bin and began to fill a small bucket with dry oats. Again David called her, but, afraid her emotions would betray her, still she did not answer.

Then he saw her standing in the far corner of the barn and walked toward her. "Cassie?" he asked with quiet concern as he placed his large hands on her shoulders and gently turned her to face him. "Is something wrong? What's happened?"

Cassie fought to control her tears as she groped to answer his question. She wanted desperately to fall into his arms and pour out the whole story of Priscilla's visit, but the very words Priscilla had uttered made her resist.

Mustering all the courage she could, she looked up and stared directly into his eyes. With a voice tinged with anger she said coldly, "What happened? You tell me." She turned quickly from him to grip the top of the adjacent stall door. Her shoulders trembled slightly as pent-up emotions gave way to silent weeping.

David looked at her questioningly, but he didn't move toward her. "If you will be more specific, maybe I can answer."

Cassie said faintly, "Priscilla Bellwood."

"Priscilla," David repeated slowly, "I'm not sure I understand—I had an appointment with her yesterday."

"Just an appointment?" Cassie asked doubtfully as she turned to face him, her eyes brimming with tears. "And just the girl you were once engaged to—and just an overnight guest at your place and just—and just—" Cassie stammered weakly as she saw the look of tenderness on David's face.

David shook his head sadly as he gently touched her cheek. "The relationship I had with Priscilla was a long time ago, when I was a different man. It is," David hesitated before finishing, "something I'm not proud of, but it's finished. I'm sorry, Cassie; I didn't mean to hurt you."

Cassie looked at David longingly, desperately wanting to believe what he had just said. "Is it really finished, David? Priscilla told me differently," she said softly.

"What do you mean?"

"She returned my yellow outfit this morning. She said you asked her to. Then she told me that you had rekindled your old relationship last night—and that you still loved her," Cassie replied with effort.

For a moment David did not stir as Cassie's words brought the full picture into focus. "I can't believe she could be that spiteful," he said, more to himself than to Cassie. "No wonder you're so upset. Priscilla lied to you about everything. I'm so sorry, Cassie, so sorry." He reached out and pulled her to his chest and held her close.

"Cassandra Delaney, I love you and you alone. I would never betray you or do anything to hurt you, and, besides," he added lightly, "I spent the night in the barn."

"I believe you, David, I believe you," Cassie said simply, as she relaxed in the harbor of his embrace.

The embrace lingered for several moments before David gently kissed Cassie on the top of her head. She raised her face to meet his and his lips brushed her forehead, then her closed eyelids, and finally rested tenderly upon her lips. They were not kisses of passion, but ones of healing and soothing, as if they sought to remove all the hurts of the last day.

David relinquished her lips, and she smiled at the caring that she saw in his eyes. "David McBride, I'm afraid you love a very foolish woman. How much simpler things would've been if I'd trusted you without question," she calmly observed.

"Maybe so," he said, "but sometimes our thinking and our feelings are easily misled."

Cassie looked at him, puzzled. "Elaborate," she requested as he sat on a bale of hay, and leaned back on a support post.

"Our mind can be so divided about something that it's hard to determine what's right and what isn't. Your mind has been divided about your feelings for me and about your career in New York. Then, when Priscilla showed up with what sounded like the truth, it was hard for your thoughts and feelings not to go along with the obvious, even though the obvious was wrong. It was easy then for you to question the sincerity of my love—and," he added slowly, "that I want you to be my wife."

Cassie paled at his last words, knowing that things were coming to a head much sooner than she wanted.

"David," Cassie said hesitantly as she felt the strain of the moment, "I realized yesterday that I do love you." She paused before continuing, hoping that he would offer a way of escape. He looked at her intently, but said nothing.

"But I don't think that's enough. I can't give up everything I've worked for to live here. Can't we compromise? There are sick people in New York too. David, I want both worlds—you and my career."

"Cassie, I love you and want you with every breath that I take. I want to care for you, to protect you. I want you by my side, to have my children, to see the good times and the bad times with me, to build a life and a love that will last forever; but God wants me here. What you're asking me to do is to choose between you and God," he stated gently.

A look of horror spread across Cassie's face. "Choose between me and God! I haven't asked you not to believe in God. I was raised in the church. I can't believe you could say something like that." Her voice lost some of its force. "David, I just think that I should choose what direction my life will take, that's all."

David looked at her with sad longing as the breach between them widened.

"For most of my life I would have agreed with what you're saying," he told her, "but, when I finally realized that part of believing in God is choosing to do what He wants, then everything in my life really began to fall into place."

Cassie sat down on an old milking stool. She placed her hands on her knees and gazed down at the dust-laden floor. Finally, she looked across at David and said with resignation, "It's no use. Even though we love each other, it just won't work. I can't live here, and you can't come to New York, and," she added unexpectedly, "I want to be in charge of my life."

David stood up slowly, as if the weight of the world rested upon his brawny shoulders. Walking over to Cassie, he knelt down on one knee and looked intently into her face. "Cassie," he began.

"I'm sorry, David. I do love you, and I don't want to lose you, but Tony called today and said there is a crisis at the magazine. I—I have to go back," she said tremulously.

David's gaze did not leave Cassie's face as the agony he felt flamed in his eyes. "Cassie, I don't want you to go, because I know that you're meant for me, but maybe now is not the time. I love you, and I'll be here waiting." Then he kissed her cheek ever so gently and turned to leave.

Cassie watched David walk toward the barn door. Her eyes did not leave his broad shoulders and the back of his sunstreaked head until the creaking old door swung shut…leaving her alone.

Chapter Eleven

Sometime before daybreak, David awoke with a grim sense of foreboding. His sleep had been restless when it finally had come just before midnight, and he still felt as tired as when he had gone to bed. He turned on the bedside lamp and looked at the clock. It was only 4:30 A.M.—early, even for him.

He got up reluctantly and stretched his long arms heavenward, yawning sleepily. He walked slowly to the dressing room with heavy feet.

David leaned over the dressing table to peer at his reflection in the mirror. He noticed dark circles under his eyes and knew that they evidenced several restless nights.

Now, David, if you don't put that woman out of your mind, you're going to be an old man at thirty-five. She's gone, but your life and work will go on, he realized, as the phantom of deep pain flickered in his somber eyes.

David turned to shower and begin the day. The memories of Cassie and her departure threatened to engulf him, but forcibly he put them aside. The warm stream of water offered a comforting balm for his tense body. Relaxing, he scrutinzed his heartache under the cold light of logic and reason.

She was gone, and he was alone. His heart yearned for the sight of those large luminous eyes, always so expressive of her inner being. He smiled as he remembered the dark orbs glowing with excitement, and at other times, stormy, reflecting a turbulence within her.

He felt an emptiness that was hard to explain. The loneliness that came from knowing that she was no longer only a couple of miles away seemed inexplicable to him. He hadn't seen her every day by any means, but contentment had come with just knowing that she was near. Now that she was no longer there, his work would have to fill that void.

The attraction to her had been hard to fight, but he had tried. From that first day, when he had stood in her kitchen looking down on her fragile loveliness, he had known that she was going to have an impact on his life. The truth of the matter was that he hadn't wanted that impact!

His life had been so fulfilled and satisfied because of his work that he never had realized the extent of his loneliness. Then Cassie had burst in and stirred his heart, filling the loneliness even as she brought it to his awareness.

David had never loved this way before. His involvement with Priscilla had been both passionate and emotional, but it had been a self-centered liaison for them both. Neither had been committed to the other's needs, and it hadn't worked. David had dismissed the idea of love and marriage, thinking that his work would be all that he needed. Then came Cassie.

She had even made his work more exciting, if that were possible. He was able to share his thoughts and dreams with her as he'd never been able to do with anyone before. Maybe that's why she had gone back to New York—those dreams had frightened her.

"I can't give them up, Cassie, not even for you, my darling," David muttered to himself as he stepped out of the shower into the quietness of the predawn morning.

The shrill ring of the telephone startled David back to the present. Any call at this early hour was not a casual one. He answered it, interrupting the second ring.

"Hello, David McBride speaking."

"David, it's Priscilla. Did I wake you up?"

"No, Priscilla, it's early, but I was awake." David's voice cooled as he recognized the voice on the other end, but his guarded look gave way to one of alarm when he heard Priscilla's message. Her voice raised to such a shrillness that it was clearly audible in the room. "David, it's your father. He's seriously ill."

"What do you mean, ill?" He asked tersely.

"We went to dinner late last evening to discuss some business, and he collapsed at the restaurant. I called an ambulance, and he's in Tournier Hospital here in St. Louis. They've diagnosed it as a massive coronary!"

David sat abruptly on the side of the bed before he could speak. Images of Dr. Jonah McBride, strong and vital, flashed before his eyes. He could see his father, trim and tan on the golf course, or playing a vigorous game of tennis. He thought of him at corporate board meetings, always alert, aggressive and probing.

As a physician, David could relate to such catastrophes and diagnose the stress that often brought them on. But, as a son, he had never entertained the idea that his father was susceptible to the pressures of life. He remembered Priscilla's admonition when she came, and it pained him to realize how long it had been since he had spent any time with Jonah.

The near-hysteria in Priscilla's voice jerked him from his reverie. "Priscilla, just calm down. I need to know the facts. Who diagnosed the heart attack? Did they run an EKG?" David asked with quiet authority.

"Yes, of course. It showed definite abnormality, so they admitted him to the coronary care unit. Oh, the doctor was Dr. Rague, the cardiologist on duty. When can you get here? He really has no one but you, and I'm frightened for him. Please come!" The normally cool Priscilla babbled on almost incoherently.

David once again tried to calm her, "Yes, Pris, I know

how much he means to you. What do they say his condition is now?"

The distraught woman took an audibly deep breath that sounded like a shudder as she answered, "They said he has stabilized some, but they don't know for how long. When will you be here?" she asked once again.

Her voice rose once more, and David was surprised to find that he felt a real compassion for this beautiful, sophisticated woman and the terror engulfing her. He knew that she sincerely cared for the elder Dr. McBride. She had never known her own father. From the first time that Priscilla had been in David's home, the little girl had latched on to the handsome, jovial patriarch. Jonah McBride always treated Priscilla as if she were the daughter he'd never had.

"Listen to me, Pris. As soon as I can get in touch with Dr. Mitchell here in town, I'll come. I'll have to call the Lexington airport to see if I can get a plane in to St. Louis; if not, I'll drive. At any rate, it will be several hours before I can make it. Isn't there anyone you can call to stay with you until I get there?"

"Uh—no. No one who would care." Priscilla's voice became strangely subdued as she stammered her revealing answer. Once again David's concern for his father was momentarily diverted, as compassion for this young woman tugged at his heart.

"Well, chin up, Prissy, I'll be there before you know it," David comforted her as he unconsciously called her by an affectionate childhood name from earlier years. "And thank you. Thank you for taking care of Dad so well," David added, realizing a surge of gratitude toward this woman with whom he had been so angry just hours earlier.

"I'll do the best I can, but hurry! He needs you; we both need you," she added, her voice finally dropping to its normal pitch, but pathetic in its message.

Within the hour David had contacted Dr. Mitchell

122

and had made arrangements for him to take emergency calls. The town doctor had offered to make rounds for David during the week, but David was relieved that none of his patients were seriously ill. Dr. Mitchell was an excellent physician, but he was in his early seventies and could not keep up with David's rigorous schedule.

David made short work of packing his bag and was soon on the road for St. Louis. His call to the Lexington airport had confirmed his doubts about available flights, so he had decided to drive.

In the late afternoon, just as rush hour hit its zenith, Big Bertha rolled into the hospital parking lot. David went straight to the entrance of the cold, austere building and climbed the stairs two at a time. He knew where he was going; he'd been here before, but in a different capacity. Now he experienced the same anxiety he had seen on the faces of his patients' families.

The waiting room was empty and fear gripped him. Priscilla should be there. Then, as he moved toward the nurses' station, he saw her standing at the window, looking out. "Priscilla," he said softly.

The slender blond whirled around as she heard her name. When she saw David, she ran toward him and flung herself into his arms. With her head buried in his jacket, she began to weep with abandon. "They think he's worse, David. I've been so afraid. Why did it take you so long?" she asked when her sobbing subsided.

"It's a long way. Where is the doctor?"

"He's in the room with Jonah now. They've had some more trouble with arrhythmia. I don't quite understand what they mean," she said.

"I'll go to the nurses' station and see what I can find out," he said, disengaging her arms and moving forward.

After a brief conversation with the floor nurse, David came back to Priscilla and said, "The doctor will see me later. I don't know a Dr. Rague; he must be new here."

"He was on duty when they admitted your dad. They

123

have called in Dr. Bennett. I believe your Dad had seen him recently."

"Chad Bennett? I know him. Fine doctor, one of the best in his field. You say Dad had been to see him?" he asked, with a puzzled look on his face.

"Yes, I told you that he wasn't feeling well," Priscilla said in a quiet manner that pierced David's heart far more than an accusation would have.

"I remember, but I didn't believe you. What was wrong with him?" he wanted to know.

"Just feeling extremely tired with a vague, uneasy feeling in his chest, was the way he described it to me, but you know our 'Mac,'" she said, "always afraid someone will think he's getting old."

"No, I never knew that about him. Fear of aging must have been a fairly recent development," David commented.

"Maybe so. I just noticed it this past year or so," Priscilla concurred.

"Here's Dr. Bennett now. Hello, Chad. Glad you're on the case. How is he?" David asked, walking across the hall and extending his hand to a tall man with dark, graying hair.

"Glad you're here, David," Chad Bennett responded as he shook David's hand. "It's hard to tell right now. It was really touch and go for several hours after he arrived. If it hadn't been for this young woman's quick thinking, Jonah wouldn't have made it."

David nodded in mute agreement as he listened to his friend. "We've had a difficult time regulating his heartbeat, but, for the last two hours, it has stabilized for the second time since he arrived. I hope this time it will stay that way."

"Can you tell how much damage has been done to the heart itself?" David queried.

"Not conclusively, but I'm sure it's extensive. You know as well as I do that it'll be seventy-two hours before we have anything more than guesses," the cardiologist responded.

"Priscilla said he'd been seeing you?"

"Yes, we'd done a thorough physical on him and he checked out fine. I noticed that he seemed under a great deal of stress, but he wouldn't talk to me about it. He just said he'd handle it," commented the older doctor. He stroked his chin absent-mindedly, trying to recall Jonah McBride's exact words. "It seemed to have something to do with his clinics—a big decision of some sort."

"I think I know what it was. Did he mention me?" David asked bluntly.

"Yes, but only this morning. At about ten o'clock he grew very restless and asked for you. He said he hoped you would come before it was too late; he *had* to talk to you. Then we sedated him heavily, and he's been asleep since."

"When can I see him?" was David's reply.

"As soon as he wakes up. I know I don't have to tell you this, David, but, if he does survive, he'll have to change his lifestyle drastically."

David looked at Dr. Chad Bennett and said with a wry smile, "I know, but with Dad that won't be easy."

"You might be surprised. I know you've observed that sometimes people see things differently after an experience like this," he responded with the hint of a smile. "Come on, let me buy you a cup of coffee. You and Ms. Bellwood both look like you could use some."

David agreed, "Come to think of it, I haven't eaten since I left home this morning, but I'd like to see your patient first, even if he is still asleep. Would you take Priscilla, and I'll join you in a few minutes."

David left the hall and slipped into the dimly lighted room. His dad was not the only patient in the room; there were several. Nurses moved about quietly and efficiently. Two nurses were seated at a console, their eyes glued to screens monitoring their patients' vital signs.

David stood at Jonah's bedside, looking down at him as he slept. He glanced up at the monitor attached to his dad and watched the rhythmic blip as it danced across the screen. It comforted him to see the steady action.

"Well, right now he's stable," he thought with a sigh of relief.

Just then the older McBride's eyes flickered open, and he saw his son.

David had feared this moment. Vivid memories of their last conversation had replayed in his mind a thousand times throughout the day and even as Chad had been speaking. How would his father react?

David searched his father's face and waited almost breathlessly. Then, with an immeasurable relief, he saw a hand reach weakly out as his dad said, "Son, I'm glad you're here."

There was no bitterness in those eyes, only a gladness—and something else David had never seen in them before. He took his parent's hand and said simply, "Me, too." The tall, strong doctor-son didn't notice that a tear had escaped, making its way down one of his cheeks.

"I need to tell you something," the older McBride murmured.

"Dad, don't. You can tell me later, when you're stronger," David soothed, with an uneasy eye turned toward the monitor.

"Yes, too weak now," Jonah agreed, closing his eyes, but still grasping his son's hand.

David stood transfixed at the bed and prayed silently. *Oh, Lord, heal the breach. Show me Your Will in this. Help me meet Dad's needs without forfeiting Your Will. Help me, Father, and please minister to him.* David opened up his own heart to be searched and cleansed of any bitterness that might be lurking within it.

Standing beside his father, David suddenly felt a love and tenderness toward the older man that he had never known before; and, with it, he knew that every vestige of resentment, even that hidden from his own awareness, had been uprooted and cast out.

Quietly, in the deep recesses of David's heart, peace gradually replaced the day's anxiety, and he now had a confidence that he couldn't explain.

When David rejoined Chad and Priscilla a few minutes later, his countenance appeared refreshed, and he looked younger by years. The change was so apparent that Priscilla commented, "David, what happened to you?"

"Relieved. I know everything's going to be all right," he explained.

Puzzled, Chad Bennett remarked, "Then you must have some knowledge I don't."

David chuckled, "Well, maybe I do, Chad, maybe I do."

The older doctor's expression grew stern as he stated firmly, "David, as a doctor you should know better than to give in to the euphoria of false hope. Jonah is critically ill and I'm not sure he's going to pull through!"

Priscilla sat in silence, her large blue eyes looking from one man to the other, as if trying to understand the exchange between the two physicians. When she heard Dr. Bennett's dire warning, her eyes filled with tears and her composure threatened to disintegrate once more.

"Chad, I'm aware of how ill my father is, and I don't know if he'll pull through or not; but I do know some of the stress he was under is gone. Wouldn't that contribute to his recovery?" David asked reasonably.

"Yes, certainly that would help. You must've talked with him," Chad said, probing for more details.

"Briefly. I knew better than to tire him," was all the explanation that he offered. "This coffee hits the spot, but I need to take Priscilla out for a breath of fresh air. Is that little Italian restaurant still down in the next block?" David asked, putting a definite end to the conversation.

"Still down there and the pizza's good as ever. It would do you both good. I'll be around the hospital for a while, and, if there's any change, I'll send somebody after you," the doctor promised.

"I don't think I can eat a bite," Priscilla remarked.

"You've got to! That's all there is to it," David countered and pulled her to her feet.

The night air was cool after the stuffy hospital, and the brisk walk refreshed David even more. When their order arrived, he realized that he was hungry.

"I'm surprised you remembered this place," Priscilla commented as she broke the stony silence that had enveloped them since they had left the hospital.

"Why? I like pizza. That's one thing I miss in the mountains; that's not standard mountain fare, you know," David quipped.

"Do you remember it for any other reason?"

"I believe we came here on our first date. Right?"

"You do remember the place, then," she said coldly.

David hesitated before he answered. Then, carefully choosing his words, he responded, "Yes, one weekend I came home from med school, and this little girl I had known for so many years had become a beautiful woman. I asked her out. Pris, I remember many things about our relationship." Then he added, without a trace of a smile, "Some good, a lot bad."

"Like what?"

"Tonight is not the time for this," he said as he turned his attention to the pizza.

The conversation ended, and, for a moment, David looked at the young woman sitting opposite him as if he were seeing her for the first time. In truth, he had never seen her like this. Her long blond hair was pulled back simply and tied with a blue ribbon. At some time during her long vigil, her makeup had disappeared, and, with it, the glamorous, successful, self-confident woman that he knew.

Even in their most intimate moments he had not seen

this Priscilla. All the facade was gone and he marveled at what it had concealed.

He realized that his feelings toward her had changed since the early morning hours, when the heat of anger had coursed through him at the sound of her voice.

David shook his head, hoping to clear it. He didn't want to deal with that right now. He had told her that tonight was not the time, yet he knew this revelation would haunt him. Priscilla Bellwood, attorney-at-law, was sharp, aggressive, calculating, and, at times, ruthless; but tonight he'd seen through her and found someone else.

"Don't you think we'd better go back to the hospital, David?" Priscilla asked.

David flinched when he realized that he had been staring. "You're probably right. Can't you eat any more than that, Prissy?"

"No, I'm ready to go. Maybe 'Mac' is awake now; and, David," she hesitated before she continued, "I'm not 'Prissy' anymore."

David paid their check, and they left. They walked in silence, neither of them even attempting any conversation.

The vigil at the hospital lasted two hours more, until the nurse came to say that Dr. McBride was awake and wanted to see them.

Priscilla went in alone for a few minutes, and e-merged looking more relaxed and encouraged. "I think you're right, David. 'Mac' seems better. He told me to go home, and I think I will. Where will you be staying?"

"I'm going to stay at the hotel next door, at least until the seventy-two hours are up."

"Then I guess I'll see you tomorrow," Priscilla said and left the room.

David stared after her for a moment, as if struggling with some decision, and then entered his father's room.

"Hi, there. You're more awake than the last time I came in," David said softly, moving closer to the bed.

He noticed that the patient's color was better and the monitor was still steady. Jonah's alertness indicated that the sedative had worn off.

"Yes, and the pain has subsided. That was pretty bad. I'm glad you're here, Son. I want to talk to you," he responded with an urgency that bothered David.

"I know you do, but I'll be around a while. We'll talk when you're stronger," David said persuasively.

"But I might not be. I'm a doctor, and I know the score. This is something that can't wait," he retorted weakly.

"OK, OK, Dad. I'm here. Tell me. I'll listen," David agreed, not wanting to upset him.

"It's just this, son. I've been wrong—wrong from the beginning," the older man stated, closing his eyes for a moment.

David moved closer to the bed in alarm. "Sir?" he asked, not understanding.

"I've been wrong—with your mother and now with you," he explained.

"What do you mean?" David still didn't fully understand what the older man was trying to tell him.

"I've chased empty dreams. Since your mother died my life has been meaningless. I thought if I opened more clinics, made more money—but that didn't help. I thought if you'd just come home and take over, then what I had accomplished would mean something." Dr. Jonah McBride paused for a few moments to catch his breath.

David said, "Dad, let's talk about it tomorrow. You're getting tired."

"No, I must tell you, now," he weakly objected. "Lying here, not knowing if I was going to make it, I realized what was wrong. My life hasn't counted; it hasn't made a lasting difference anywhere," he haltingly explained.

"That's not true. You made Mom happy, Dad," David argued.

"But she's gone," Jonah said.

"Well, you still have me," his son reminded him.

"That's my point. *I don't*. I *lost* you somewhere in my drive to get ahead. I thought I wanted the success for you and your mother, but she didn't need my success, and you didn't want it. I realized that my life could've counted if I'd invested it where God wanted me to—in people. Then I decided it might not be too late. Whether I make it or not, I want to set up your clinic for you. That's what I had to tell you."

David was too stunned to say anything at first. He just took his father's hand and squeezed it gently. Then, when he brought his emotions under control, he asked, "Dad, are you sure this is what you want to do?"

"Sure of two things: that God wants me to do this and that I want to. That way my financial success can be invested in something that will have lasting value. You see, I had to tell you this tonight. Now I'm tired. You come back tomorrow, and we'll work out the details later. Good night, son." With that, Jonah let out a deep sigh, as if a heavy weight had been lifted.

When David left the room, his emotions were running rampant. Joy flooded him within because the breach had been healed, but he was having difficulty comprehending his father's decision about the Appalachian clinic.

David made his way to the hotel and arranged for a room for the next three nights. After a quick shower, he threw his exhausted body across the bed, and, just as he dropped into a deep sleep, he saw in his mind's eye the pair of expressive dark eyes in a lovely oval face. "Cassie," he murmured as he felt an overwhelming desire to share with her the heartaches and joys of this unusual day. That was the last thought David McBride had before he slept the sleep of one who is at peace with the world and his God.

David's father survived the critical period and grew stronger. When Dr. Bennett was convinced that his condition had stabilized, he moved the patient to a large, private suite. He confirmed his earlier, grim assessment of Dr. "Mac's" condition when tests came back showing extensive heart damage.

The older McBride took the news with a calmness that surprised David, despite their earlier conversation. On the fourth day after his attack, he requested to see Priscilla and David together.

The couple arrived at the room simultaneously, and Priscilla asked David if he knew what provoked the summons. "He called me early this morning and told me I was to be here no later than 8:30 and bring a pad and tape recorder. Is he worse?" Priscilla asked, as she told David about the strange call. "He told me that you were to be here. Does that mean you have changed your mind about taking over your father's business?"

David avoided answering her question. "Here we are, I guess we'll both know soon."

David was amazed at the change in his father's appearance. He had exchanged his hospital gown for blue silk pajamas with a navy, monogrammed robe pulled over them. He still was attached to a monitor, but his color had improved, and he was noticeably stronger.

Jonah was drinking a cup of coffee, and David raised an inquiring eyebrow. "Who did you bribe for that?"

"No one; it's decaffeinated. Not very good, but better than nothing."

Priscilla broke in, "You look better. I'm glad to see that you got out of your hospital designer gown; it didn't do a thing for you."

The older McBride smiled affectionately at the young woman, immaculately dressed in an ivory linen suit. The signs of fatigue and disarray of four days ago had disappeared, and once again she was the epitome of a career woman at her loveliest.

"Priscilla, I wanted you to take care of some legal matters for me. I've decided that I'm going to finance David's clinic. I want you to make the legal arrangements."

"You what?" the question exploded from her.

"You heard me. This is the way I want to handle it. I'm going to sell my clinics. All the proceeds, except for your fee, will go toward that. I want a trust set up to take care of it now and later."

Priscilla's blue eyes had turned to ice as she shifted her gaze from father to son. Thus far David had made no comment, and the news obviously hadn't surprised him. "As your attorney I must advise you against this foolish move."

"Why is it foolish, Pris?"

"Because you've worked too hard to throw it all away like this!" Priscilla clamped her teeth together in an attempt to stem the heated argument erupting within her.

"In the first place, I can live comfortably without those clinics, and what good do they really do anyway?"

"They've been very profitable."

"In dollars and cents, you mean?" Mac asked.

"Isn't that what it's all about?" Priscilla retorted.

"Priscilla, I don't expect you to agree or understand; I'm just directing you to follow my instructions. I want a power of attorney issued to David so that he can act in my stead. Give him your every cooperation in disposing of these clinics, do you understand?" Jonah's voice was firm and resolute. "That's all I wanted, so, if you'll get to work on these details, I'll take a nap like a good patient," he said in an abrupt dismissal and turned his back to them.

"Well, David, I guess you win! Don't you think it was a little unethical to pressure your dad while he's in this condition?" an angry Priscilla asked David after they had left the hospital room.

"I know you'll find this hard to believe, but I had nothing to do with his decision," David responded mildly.

"You're right. I don't believe you. You're just like everybody else! When you see your chance, you go for it, no matter what. I guess you know this will ruin him.

Why does he want to sell his clinics? Can't he just donate the funds?"

He laughed softly. "Pris, you'll never understand. I didn't change his mind and it won't ruin him. It will *save* him."

"Ha, there you go again, more of that high-and-mighty religious stuff. No thank you, Dr. McBride; I've seen how you operate—wait for the right opportunity and dive in for the kill," she said as she raised her voice heatedly.

"I wasn't talking about 'high-and-mighty religious stuff,' as you put it. I'm talking about an old man who wants to exchange an unfulfilling life for a fulfilled one, that's all."

"Who says his life is unfulfilled? He's made a fortune, hasn't he?" she countered.

"Yes, and now he wants to invest it in something that will live on after him. Believe me, that's a decision that I would never have persuaded him to make," David explained patiently.

"I guess you realize this decision will also ruin me. He's my biggest account. David, how can you throw away everything your Dad has accomplished and ruin me at the same time?"

"In the first place, I'm not going to throw anything away. That's why I have agreed to stay until we find a buyer for the clinics. As for ruining you, that's not true. You'll be the attorney for Dad's other holdings, and you know they're extensive. Besides that, our foundation will need legal counsel and perhaps, if you ever see any value in it, you might want to provide that," David said calmly.

Priscilla remained quiet for a moment as David watched the struggle in her eyes. The calculating look of one taking in a new situation and turning it to her advantage struggled with another, more subtle expression. David was fascinated, waiting to see the outcome.

When Priscilla spoke, the words came from the Priscilla that he had glimpsed four nights ago behind the makeup. "What if I did decide there was value in what you're doing? Would that make a difference between us?"

He looked at her intently as he weighed his words carefully. He saw into the heart of a young woman who desperately needed someone to love her, one who had covered her vulnerability with the hard, cold veneer of success, but who would never be satisfied with anything else. "Priscilla, you know you couldn't be happy in Kentucky. *This* is your world."

"But would it change things between us, David?" she persisted.

David took her hand and looked sadly into her eyes as he recognized the strange emotion he had felt toward her in the restaurant four nights ago. Finally he was free from the strong attraction to her which had bound him for years, and, in its place, he felt compassion and remorse. He answered her gently, "No, Pris. The love I have for you is not the kind you need. You will always have a special place in my heart. We grew up together and shared an intimacy, even though wrong, that will remain in my memory. But we don't have the kind of love on which to build a relationship. We didn't before, and we don't now. I can only ask your forgiveness for the pain I've caused you."

"I don't know what you mean, David. As far as I'm concerned, our relationship was not wrong. Our only problem then and now is your love for those back hills of Kentucky," she retorted, as the suave sophisticate once again took control. "Perhaps you're right. If I play my cards right and get a good buyer for the clinics it can do nothing but good for my career. Of course, we'll have to go to New York to find what we need. You know I have some contacts there. Will you stay until everything is settled?" she asked, all business.

"I'm committed to staying. One of the young men at Dad's clinic is interested in my work, and I'm sending him home to stand in for me," David declared.

Chapter Twelve

Cassie asked not to be announced before she entered Tony's office in New York. He was behind his desk, partially turned toward the window. All she could see was part of his profile; but she knew that, if she were face to face with him, his eyes would be narrowed, with dark circles under them and a slight wrinkle in his brow. Tony was under stress.

"Tony," she said softly.

He whirled around, but, when he saw her, the expression on his face relaxed. "Cassandra! Well, you did come back. Glad to see you, Darling. I knew you couldn't stay away." He moved around the desk toward her.

"I guess you know me pretty well. What's the big crisis?"

"We'll talk about that later. Let me look at you. You look different. Softer or something; you've cut your hair. I like it, only it makes you look younger." Tony pulled her over to the window to get a better look. "Yes, I think your 'vacation' did you good. So you finished your book, eh?"

"Yes, and I'm pleased with it."

"I can't wait to read it. Where would you like to dine tonight?" he asked abruptly.

"Dinner, tonight?"

"Yes, anywhere—you name it!"

Cassie stared at him for a long moment, then smiled

but answered firmly, "Tony, have you forgotten your promise so soon? I came back because you said the magazine needed me. I didn't come back to you. There will be no dinner tonight *or any other night*."

"I don't believe you mean that," he smiled as he reached for her.

Cassie resisted and stepped back, pushing him away. She looked up directly into his eyes. "It's this way, Tony. If you need me here at the magazine, you leave me alone, and, if you don't, I'll be on my way. What was between us is over, a finished chapter, and I want that clearly understood before I set one foot in my office."

Tony looked at her in amazement. "You don't know what you're saying, Cassandra; do you know what you're risking?"

"Yes, nothing. If there's a job to be done here, and you need me, fine. If not, then I'll get another, simple as that. It's up to you. Those are my terms."

"You're telling me you want your job, but you don't want me?"

"That's exactly right!"

Tony hesitated a moment, then began to laugh. "When you get your little feathers ruffled, they're really ruffled. All right, my love, have it your way. You'll cool off. Anyway, we've got too much work to worry about our personal involvement. There will have to be *some* socializing, 'though. We've got some accounts to win back, and no one can beat the team of Saikas and Delaney in that department."

"Suppose you start from the beginning and tell me what our problems are."

"I explained some of it on the phone, but the end results are lost advertisers, lost subscribers, angry authors, low staff morale, and a Board of Directors on the warpath!"

"That's hard for me to understand. The magazine layouts were planned months in advance. I had scheduled every article when I left."

"That's our problem; Hilary canceled your decisions and formated new stuff that was inferior and offensive."

"Why did you let her get by with it?"

"I didn't know it!"

"Why not?"

"Because I went on a vacation to Cannes. Why didn't *you* notice it? Didn't you get the magazine every month?"

The truth of the question ripped away any blame she might place on him. "Yes, but I didn't read it. I wanted to forget it."

Tony sighed, "Too late to cry over spilled milk. It's time to roll up our sleeves and get to work."

Truly, Cassie had no worry about personal relationships in the days that followed. Neither she nor Tony had any time beyond what they could give to their work. Their work days were twelve to eighteen hours long, and their weeks were six and seven days. They were bound in a common goal—saving the magazine.

Cassie salvaged her plans for the remaining months. She wrote to disgruntled authors, promising the publication of their work in a later issue, or apologizing and sending them a "kill fee" if she couldn't use their articles.

She had staff breakfasts weekly to improve morale. And gradually, as she brought some semblance of order to the chaos that had ruled, she won back the Board of Directors' confidence.

True to his word, Tony required her to attend numerous—but innocuous—luncheons and parties with him in an attempt to woo back their lost accounts.

Her charm, beauty, and expertise proved invaluable and, little by little, the accounts came trickling back in to the *Woman's Life* coffers.

Cassie had never worked so hard or so desperately, but she relished the challenge. It offered her an escape from the haunting memories she had left behind in Kentucky. She didn't have time to think of David as her mind plotted, planned, and executed the frenzied activities destined to save the publication. At night when she finally went to bed, she slept the deep sleep of exhaustion.

She had been back at work six weeks when Tony came down one morning from his suite to her office. He walked in unannounced and nonchalantly wandered around as she sat watching him with cool amusement.

"How about a new office?" he asked.

"This one's fine. Can I help you with something?"

"What makes you think I want something?" he responded.

"The mountain doesn't usually come to Mohammed," she quipped with growing amusement.

"There's an office available right next to mine."

"No, thanks."

"Come on, Cassie, you're being ridiculous," he said testily.

"Do you really think I need a new office?"

"Yes. That's what I came down here to talk to you about. It looks like I'm going to have to go to Paris if we save the Chelva account. You're going to have to take over some of my duties while I'm away. This office just won't do."

"Does it have a window?" she asked.

"One whole wall is glass."

"OK, when do I move?"

Tony smiled broadly. "As soon as you want to."

"By the way, I think you're right about the Chelva account—you don't need me on that one. You've been their sole contact."

"No, you forgot Hilary. That's my problem—I let her handle it after you left."

Cassie shrugged her shoulders. "When will you leave?"

139

"Tonight. I have a midnight flight. How about having dinner with me?"

"Sorry, but you know the rules."

"This is business. I have appointments all afternoon, so that will be the only time I can go over some of these details with you," he explained.

Cassie considered it for a minute and then said, "I guess you're right. My schedule is full, too. Where shall I meet you, and what time? My last appointment is at four."

"I'll pick you up at your apartment around seven and that should give us plenty of time."

Promptly at seven, Tony rang her doorbell. Cassie opened her door and let herself out without inviting him in. "I thought you wouldn't have time to come in," she said in a half-hearted explanation.

"No, our reservation is at seven-fifteen. By the way, you look enchanting." His eyes traveled appreciatively from the dark curls framing her face to her large eyes, full lips, and down to the hem of her short black evening dress.

Cassie looked stunning in black and the simple lines of the expensive dress accented every feminine curve. The only jewelry she wore was her grandmother's diamond-and-sapphire pendant that sparkled as it lay on the filmy material draping her neck.

Tony smiled slyly and offered her his arm. "It'll be difficult to concentrate on business when you look like that."

"I'll change if you like. Jeans, maybe, and a flannel shirt?" She raised an eyebrow with a mischievous look.

"I don't think they would let you in at Sayora's dressed like that. Anyway, don't forget that image you have to maintain," he laughed.

"I'm glad we're going to Sayora's. I've read good reviews about the place but just haven't had time to try it out."

Dusk had fallen when Cassie and Tony arrived at their

destination. The doorman opened the door for Cassie, and she stepped out just as Tony reached her side of the car. She paused and looked upward. This was one of the newer additions to Manhattan's skyline. It spiraled upward for fifty floors of bronze and glass. There was a courtyard in front of the building featuring a modern bronze sculpture.

They walked through revolving doors and across a marble lobby to an elevator that whisked them to the top through a glass tube on the outside of the building. The view of the city was spectacular.

From their table next to a window, Cassie could see New York outlined against the last pink brush-strokes of a lingering sunset. The lights of the city twinkled like stars—and, without warning, uninvited memories of *another* view deluged Cassie's mind. The magnificence of this one faded as she yearned for the sights and sounds of another, simpler place.

The waiter interrupted her thoughts and she looked at Tony and said, "Why don't you order for me? I don't know what I want." Her memories left her with no appetite. She looked around her at the elegant furnishings—the glass dome where the stars shone through; the finely crafted, candlelit tables; the ornate silver flatware; and the Wedgewood china. She saw everything to enhance a fine meal, while, in the background, a chamber orchestra played soft, romantic music. Everything needed for an enjoyable evening was here...

Everything but David, her heart cried out.

"Cassandra, are you all right?" Tony Saikas asked with a look of concern on his face.

"Of course. Why?"

"I just asked you the same question three times. You haven't answered me yet."

"Wool gathering, I guess," was the only explanation that she would give him.

"Not very pleasant by the look on your face. Want to tell Uncle Tony all about it?"

"Uncle Tony?" she laughed, dispelling her somber mood.

"That's more like it; but, seriously, I'm here if you need someone to talk to," he said gently.

Cassie's mind whirled as she tried to evaluate this new approach. *Was it possible? Had Tony changed?* she wondered. "Thank you, Tony, but this is a private matter and something I've got to work out. Now let's get down to business."

Tony searched her face and, when he could get no answers from her, said, "Yes, we do have a lot to cover."

They spent two hours over their meal as they discussed and plotted the course that the magazine was to take while he was away. Tony briefed Cassie on all business and administrative affairs that were unfamiliar to her. The dinner turned out just as he had promised—purely business.

They left the restaurant at nine-thirty and had time for a leisurely drive to Cassie's apartment. When they arrived at the front door, she told him he need not see her inside. As Tony leaned across to open the car door for her, he picked up her hand and said, "You see, Cassie, things still can be good between us. Tonight was like old times."

Cassie watched his car as it drove away and thought, *It can never be like old times again, Tony. Because that was before David.*

That was the first night since Cassie had been back in New York that she cried herself to sleep.

A despondent Cassie stood on the twenty-eighth floor of Hamilton Towers and looked out the window of her expensive, new office at a smog-filled June sky. The old thrill of accomplishment was missing. The crisis that Tony had called her to avert was finally settled and to their advantage.

It was now mid-June and the magazine was running smoothly again. Tony would be home soon with a new

142

contract from Chelva, and, with that, their final lost account would be recouped. She finally had time to breathe a sigh of relief and relish her victories, but the joy refused to come. Her thoughts were only painful, bittersweet memories of what she had left back in Kentucky.

Oh, David, where has the joy in my work gone? I can't blame it on Tony. He hasn't even been here. It's been my greatest triumph—yet it's so empty. Why? Was my decision to come back wrong? If you really loved me, why haven't you called?

The final proofs of her book had not excited her. Each time she picked up the pages, her heart ached as David's face swam before her and she rememberd his touch, that crooked smile, his words of love and sharing. She had been afraid—afraid of losing what she had here in New York. She had thought that David wouldn't be enough. Now she was back and the emptiness was worse than ever.

Angie Nowlin, her new assistant, interrupted her introspection. "Ms. Delaney, Mrs. Saikas wants to see you in her office if you're free."

Cassie knew that an invitation from Tony's mother was a summons. She looked at her calendar and told Angie to cancel her appointments for the next two hours, and left to enter the private elevator that would take her to the executive penthouse office suite.

"Come in, Cassandra," the slender, gray-haired woman with cat-like eyes greeted her and stared a moment, as if inspecting every detail of Cassie's appearance. Then, with a nod of approval, she asked her to be seated. "There are several things I want to discuss with you today. First of all, your book is not what we thought it was going to be." Delphine Hamilton Saikas paused and looked over her half-glasses to observe Cassie's reaction.

Cassie returned her gaze steadily. "That's right, but it's a lot better than what I originally planned."

"This may surprise you, Cassandra, but I agree with you. It's a definite departure from what we've been publishing, but I think it has possibilities. We're going to take a big gamble and go all out on the promotional campaign. How would you like to have a bestseller?" She finished with a smile that warmed her cold green eyes.

"That would be gratifying. I appreciate your confidence in it and me, and I don't think you'll be disappointed," Cassie responded.

"I've taken the liberty of making an appointment for the two of us for lunch at Jerome's. Will that fit your schedule?"

"Of course," Cassie responded, recognizing the casual question as a directive to arrange her schedule accordingly. "My schedule is flexible today. When shall we leave?"

"Right away. I've called for the car."

Soon they were seated in the soft leather seats of the silver, chauffeured limousine as it made its way slowly down the crowded Manhattan streets.

The car stopped in front of an older building whose facade was reminiscent of the elaborate brickwork done in the early nineteen hundreds. The building stood only ten stories high, dwarfed by the surrounding ones. Cassie had to restrain a gasp when she entered and found herself in the most elegant room she had ever seen.

Above Cassie's head was a brilliant chandelier of brass and cut glass; beneath it was a floor of highly polished marble forming a hexagon, surrounded with a soft green plush carpet. The furniture was walnut, Queen Anne style, and Cassie couldn't decide if the pieces were genuine antiques or reproductions.

Delphine Saikas suggested the quiche, and, when it came, it lived up to her recommendation. After they had finished and were waiting for their coffee, the publisher said, "Cassandra, I understand that you're working without a contract. I know Tony didn't have time to pursue this with you before he left, so I thought I would take care of this little item for him while he's gone. It was good of you to work without one."

"No, Mrs. Saikas, you misunderstand. I didn't want one," she quietly corrected.

"Now, my dear, you must be mistaken. Surely you realize the chance you are taking. You have no job security whatsoever without a written contract."

"My job security is in my performance. Do you have any complaints about it?"

"No, of course not. We'd just like to have things official—say, a five-year contract?"

"No, I'm sorry, but I don't want a five-year contract," was the brief response.

"At double your present wage and a substantial bonus thrown in each year, based on your circulation increases and advertising output?" The gray-haired lady smiled smugly, certain that Cassie couldn't refuse that generous offer.

The enormity of the offer momentarily stunned Cassie. She knew that, in terms of success, she had made it. This offer would put her at the top of her field. For a moment, she was heady with the concept. Then, strangely, something inside her recoiled from the idea. She met the other woman's green eyes directly and said, "I'm overwhelmed with the offer, but I can't accept."

Disbelief spread over Delphine's aristocratic face. "Cassandra, do you have any idea what you're turning down?" Then she probed, "Does my son have anything to do with this? Has he been difficult to work with? If so, I can take care of that right away."

"We've had our differences in the past, but none since I returned."

"I thought at one time maybe you two were getting serious. Is that true?" The green eyes, usually so cold, now burned with intensity as she questioned Cassie.

145

"I don't think that's relevant," she quickly answered.

"If it's of any importance to you, we would welcome you as a daughter-in-law! In fact, I think it's time that Tony settled down, and I've observed you carefully. You have the qualities he needs," she said matter-of-factly.

Cassie suppressed a bitter smile. "Don't you think that's for Tony to decide? The last I heard, marriage wasn't in his vocabulary!"

"Oh, so that's it. Well, my dear, men have been known to change their minds," Delphine said as she signed the check which the waiter presented.

"That isn't the question anymore." Cassie fought to keep her temper under control. "You see, I don't want a contract, and I'm not interested in marrying Tony."

A frown briefly flickered across the older woman's face. It was replaced by a confident smile as she said, "I understand. You've been hurt; time has a way of healing all things. You'll see things differently soon."

Cassie started to object when a familiar voice interrupted her by calling her name. She turned to her right and saw the slender form of beautiful, blond Priscilla Bellwood! She had just entered the restaurant with three men. They were deeply engrossed in conversation when Priscilla said something to them and walked across the room toward the two women. Memories of their last meeting surged through Cassie, blotting out her momentary anger. When Cassie spoke, her calm voice belied the inner tumult which this encounter provoked. "Hello, Priscilla. Mrs. Saikas, this is Priscilla Bellwood. *Woman's Life* did a feature on her last year."

"Oh, yes. I've known Priscilla for several years. I'm the one who suggested her to Tony for the article. What brings you East this time?" Delphine asked.

"Business. Some legal matters concerning one of my clients' investments," she answered the older woman. Turning to Cassie, she said with a sly smile, "In fact, my client was a former neighbor of Cassandra's in Kentucky. Did you know Dr. McBride is back in St. Louis?"

Cassie maintained her calm exterior. "No, I didn't. I've been busy and haven't had time to keep in touch."

Priscilla smiled sweetly and added, "He decided to take his dad's offer after all."

The half-lie hit its mark. It seemed like an eternity before Cassie could respond. When her words came, they were faultless, but not before the naked pain in her eyes was visible to both women, giving victory to one and food for thought to the other. "That is a surprise, but whatever he does I wish him well."

"I'll give him your message when I see him tonight," Priscilla responded. "Now I must get back to my friends. It was really nice seeing you." Priscilla turned from them with a triumphant gleam in her eye and strode away.

The two women engaged in very little conversation on the drive back to the office. The pain Priscilla had caused Cassie reached a crescendo by the time the sleek car pulled up to the door. She managed to get out of the car and mumble some courteous words to her employer before she escaped to the dubious sanctuary of her desk. Delphine Hamilton Saikas stood looking at the retreating figure of the young editor with a questioning look in her eyes.

The compressed schedule that greeted Cassie when she returned to her desk did not alleviate her painful thoughts. She stared at the pile of promising new manuscripts that had filtered in. She opened the first one and began to read. The words had no meaning as the face of David swam between her and the page. His voice seemed real as she heard him say, "This is the place God wants me, Cassie. I'll be here waiting."

She was lying again. That must be it. She lied before, and she'd lie again. But why haven't I heard from David? If he really loved me, wouldn't he have contacted me, at least written a letter? She vacillated between hope and complete despair. Finally, she picked up the phone and dialed a familiar number.

As the connection was made, she could imagine the ring sounding throughout the large house, and she waited impatiently for that familiar voice to answer.

"Hello, Dr. McBride's residence," a deep voice answered.

Cassie's heart leaped with joy when she heard the voice, only to crash in bitter disappointment with the realization that is was *not* David's.

"Could I speak with Dr. McBride, please?"

"I'm sorry, he isn't here. Could I help you?" asked the voice.

"When do you expect him?" was the curt reply.

"I don't. He's in St. Louis. I'm Dr. Michaels. Perhaps I could help you," the doctor offered.

Sadly, Cassie put the receiver back in its cradle without an answer. She picked up the manuscripts and left the office through her private entrance, without even telling Angie to cancel her afternoon appointments. For the first time in Cassandra Delaney's career, her work lost all meaning for her. Her heart was breaking, and she took time to mourn.

Chapter Thirteen

Three weeks passed and Cassie went about her tasks woodenly. She had cried until there were no more tears to cry. She buried herself once more in her work. It still seemed meaningless, but the routine helped the days to go by and, at night, she read manuscripts until she was so tired she fell into a fitful sleep.

She had thought that Tony had hurt her, but nothing could compare with this present pain. Although she had rejected David's love and chosen her career instead, the knowledge that he was there waiting had been a source of comfort that subconsciously had sustained her.

She had fallen in love with a man of strong principle and commitment. How could his words have been lies? She knew that the deep, abiding peace that David had was genuine, so how could his devotion to God be a sham?

What had happened? There must be a good explanation, or was her judge of character that faulty? She had been wrong about Tony—perhaps about David, too?

"But Pop believed in David," she said as she reached for the phone and began to dial.

The phone rang several times as Cassie impatiently waited for Aubry to answer.

"Hello," came the crusty voice at the other end.

"Pop, I was afraid I'd missed you. I wanted to see how you're doing." Cassie delayed while she struggled for courage to ask about David.

"Well, girl…it's 'bout time you was checking in. I miss hearing yur voice, like I use ta. How are things up there?"

"Oh, fine. I miss you, too…and…ah..I just wondered what people were doing for a doctor, now that David's in St. Louis?" Cassie asked, trying to sound casual.

"How'd ya know Doc was gone?"

Not wanting to tell Pop of her meeting with Priscilla, she said simply. "I just met one of his old friends who said he was back in St. Louis."

"Well, he shore hated to leave us…but with his Pa being so sick and all…he jest didn't have no choice. He did get a feller, a Doc Michaels to come take his place. He's a-doing okay…but he shore ain't Doc."

Cassie for a brief moment felt relief at Pop's words. It was short-lived.

"We sure miss him, but I just don't know if he's ever goin' to make it back to us. He's in a bad spot, not knowing what to do, or where his duty is."

After her talk with Pop, Cassie tried to put her heartache into some sort of perspective. She understood why David had left, but the thought of his staying in St. Louis with Priscilla kept her heart from healing.

She was still by the phone when it rang. As soon as she picked up the receiver, she heard the familiar voice of Tony Saikas saying, "Can you meet me at the airport? I'm coming home."

"Tell me if it's with or without the Chelva account, then I'll tell you if I'll meet you," she ventured.

"You're a tough one, Cassandra. Yes, we've got the account back plus two others! How about that for a successful 'man-about-town'?"

"I'm sure you've been that all right," she observed sardonically.

Hours later, Tony came through the terminal gate with a confident stride and a broad grin. When he reached Cassie, he gave her a long look, "What's happened to you, my love?"

"Why do you ask that?"

"You're pale, and pardon the criticism, you're thin as a rail."

"I haven't had time for sunbathing, you know," she said evasively.

"There's more to it than that. I shouldn't have dumped this whole business on you. Has my mother been giving you problems?"

"She's been a lamb. Couldn't have been more encouraging."

"Then what's wrong?"

"Some personal problems I'm trying to work out," Cassie admitted weakly, dropping her head so Tony couldn't see the tears that filled her eyes.

"Cassie," Tony said as he put his hand under her chin and lifted her head up, "I told you before I left, I'm here if you need me."

"Thanks, Tony, but I'll manage."

"Very well. I won't press, but I do think you need a break. How about going to that new show that opens tonight? I read the reviews on the plane, and they said it was outstanding on the road, especially the Boston performance."

Cassie almost turned him down, but the image of Priscilla and David together in St. Louis flashed through her mind and she responded with determination, "Yes, I think I'd like that."

Cassie pulled her long evening gown over her head, carefully trying to keep her hair in place. She had taken the afternoon off and gone to the hair salon. Her dark tresses had grown long enough to pile high on her head with wisps of curly tendrils escaping to frame her face here and there.

The deep rose of her dress complimented her dark beauty and she wore a little more makeup than usual to cover her pallor. She looked in the mirror and noticed that the long, slim skirt revealed her slenderness, but not to her disadvantage. He recent weight loss accented her cheek bones, and her eyes looked enormous in her small face.

The reflection in the mirror satisfied her, and she felt a hint of excitement about the evening ahead. The gala opening promised to be an entertaining diversion.

The show lived up to their expectations. It was a musical comedy, well written and superbly acted. Just before the final curtain, Cassie admitted to herself that she had enjoyed the evening.

Tony had been pleasantly attentive and undemanding. Their earlier dinner had been delicious and the show outstanding. She applauded enthusiastically as the cast took seven curtain calls.

The house lights came on, and she and Tony stood up, filing into the moving crowd. As they reached the lobby, they were discussing an amusing scene when Cassie dropped her jacket. She walked a few steps before she missed it. Just as she turned from Tony to look for it, the crowd separated them and a long arm reached out to hand it to her.

She looked up in appreciation and straight into the face of David McBride!

Their eyes met in startled recognition as a cool, feminine voice said, "Why, look who's here! I didn't recognize you, Cassandra. Did you, David?"

Cassie stood frozen to the floor as she took in Priscilla Bellwood, a blonde vision in a long, black gown which bared one shoulder and clung sensuously to her every curve as she hung possessively on David's arm.

"Yes, I'd know her anywhere," he said softly, his eyes not leaving her face.

By this time, Tony had maneuvered his way back to Cassie's side. Recognizing Priscilla, he said, "Hello, Priscilla, what are you doing here?" He gave her an appreciative glance. "Gorgeous as ever, I see."

"David and I were so eager to see this show while we were in town. He did some arm-twisting to get us tickets, and here we are. Oh, by the way, David, this is Tony Saikas. You know, of *Woman's Life*."

David's eyes left Cassie's as he heard Tony's name. "So you're Tony," he murmured.

"Well, yes, that's right, but I believe you have me at a disadvantage. You're—?" Tony stammered.

"David McBride, from Kentucky," he cut in.

"You mean St. Louis, darling," Priscilla crooned.

"Glad to meet you, McBride. Have you met Cassandra?"

"A long time ago," he remarked, as his attention once more focused on Cassie.

Cassie did not move or respond. Her whole being had turned to ice. There he was, handsome and resplendent in evening wear just as she had known he would be—those same blue eyes that had melted her heart; the mouth that had smiled a crooked grin and kissed her so tenderly; the strong arms that had held her close—and all in the firm grasp of Priscilla Bellwood.

Cassie finally dropped her eyes and stammered, "Thank you for returning my jacket, Dr. McBride," as she turned to walk away, leaving an astonished Tony to make a brief farewell and follow.

She did not speak a word as they made their way to the car. Like someone in a trance, she ignored Tony's attempts at conversation. They traveled through the late night streets in silence until Tony pulled up in front of her apartment building.

"Cassandra, something is going on here that I don't understand. You were fine until we ran into Priscilla and Dr. McBride. What happened?"

With that question, a deluge broke loose and Cassie told Tony between sobs about her love for David.

Tony listened quietly to a Cassie he'd never seen before. The composure that always had surrounded her dissolved in a torrent of tears. He patted her hand like a sympathetic friend, and, in the darkness, Cassie could not see his lip curl in anger or his eyes burn with jealousy. She was too distraught to notice anything but the pain that racked her. In the theater lobby she had experienced a moment of truth she would never forget. The decision to come back to New York had been wrong, and she had lost David!

Almost a month had passed since her encounter with David. Cassie found herself remembering what Mrs. Saikas had said at their luncheon meeting—time heals.

Time doesn't always heal, Cassie thought, *but it can make a difference.*

She knew that her heart had not mended, but, as the weeks passed, she deliberately forced her grief and longing for David into the deep recesses of her being. In its place a new solidity was formed, a protective covering of hard veneer that refused to let any past emotions surface.

Time was on her side, she mused as she continued to deny her mind access to any thought of David.

Her survivor's instinct recognized her career as her only option and she went forth seeking new horizons to conquer, new tasks to perform—all with a misdirected zeal. The magazine expanded and diversified. Cassie and Tony even made plans to branch out with the creation of another magazine.

The question of a work contract surfaced once again and this time she listened with a new interest. Yet, in the final decision, she could not bring herself to commit to the five years they were asking.

How odd, she reflected. *My career is my life, but* ....she didn't finish the thought as she remembered the look of alarm on Mrs. Saikas's face and her words to Tony. "Cassandra," Delphine had suggested boldly, "maybe Tony could persuade you. What do you think, son? Doesn't that sound like an interesting challenge?"

154

Tony had looked at his mother's intense gaze and responded. "A challenge I look forward to."

The contract had not been mentioned again as the weeks passed and the work schedule became even more hectic. Cassie continued to immerse herself in her career and to deny her emotions. There was no acknowledgement, even to herself, of the depth of her own unhappiness and need.

Gradually her relationship with Tony underwent a subtle change. It had begun a few days after she had broken down and told him of her love for David. Now and then he would send her a single red rose with a simple, encouraging word, and he always seemed to be there when she needed an understanding ear.

Cassie slowly allowed their business engagements to evolve into social affairs. She enjoyed Tony's company as a much-needed diversion and, surprisingly, his treatment of her had continued to be undemanding.

Cassie had failed to recognize her emotional vulnerability as everything within her responded to Tony's caring "hands-off" attitude. He was gentle, thoughtful, concerned—and they did have the bond of a common professional goal.

One evening, as they were driving home from a late business dinner, Cassie was astonished when Tony picked up her hand and asked casually, "Don't you think it's time for us to team up for real?"

"Team up? I thought we were a team," she said, puzzled.

"No, Cassie, I mean as Mr. and Mrs. Tony Saikas."

Cassie's eyes bulged in disbelief. "You know I can't do that."

"Why not?" he asked.

"I don't love you."

"So? You will as soon as you get McBride out of your system, and that'll be soon—You were in love with a myth. I'm real, Cassie, and you need me. We're good together," was his simple explanation.

"I thought you didn't believe in marriage!"

"I was wrong. Marriage to you is what I want and what you need. I can take care of you. I'd never be a hindrance to your career, and with me your opportunities would be limitless. You don't love me—so what? Love's only an emotion. No, what we've got is better than that—we're good for each other. Together we make things happen."

"This is very flattering, Tony—but I can't give you an answer tonight," she hedged, her mind whirling. As a moth dances toward the flame, Cassandra tentatively entertained thoughts of a marriage of convenience.

"Cassandra, I can't understand why you think it's really necessary to make this trip to Kentucky to ask your caretaker's blessing before you'll decide to marry me," Tony balked.

"Pop's the nearest thing I have to a family—or father. I guess in some ways I'm traditional—I want Pop to meet you."

"Oh, I'd like to meet Mr. Bailey too, but does this mean you're going to want the white veil, preacher, and all?"

"Who knows? I might."

Cassie was as puzzled as Tony about why she really wanted to make this trip—or why she hadn't told Pop that they were coming. Her mind was made up, even though she hadn't given Tony a definite answer. *She was going to marry him.* He had been right—love could come later. After all, she'd thought she loved him once, until David. Maybe what she felt for David was just an illusion. Anyway, she couldn't have made him happy, and now he was back in St. Louis. Dr. McBride was a closed chapter in her life; no need for her to look back. She might as well face it—she was like Tony. They wanted the same things in life; their goals were more compatible.

Then, from out of the recesses of her mind, a scene

played before her of a picnic by a splendorous waterfall and of David's holding her and saying, "But are you happy, Cassie? Are you happy?" For a moment the replay was so real that Cassie unconsciously touched her lips to see if the warmth of his springtime kiss was still there. She shuddered as she realized what she had done.

"Cassandra, Cassandra, what's wrong? You're a million miles away!" came Tony's insistent voice as he watched her in bewilderment.

"Oh, nothing, nothing at all...I was just thinking about Kentucky and how surprised Pop will be when we drive up this weekend. I thought we could fly to Louisville and then rent a car and drive to the farm. Is that all right with you, Tony?"

Tony said nothing, but watched her closely as he weighed her words. "I'm not quite sure if you were telling me the truth a moment ago, but yes, I think we can make it this weekend. If my meeting Mr. Bailey is that important to you, then that's what I want, too."

"You'll like him. He's not polished...very homespun...and plain-spoken...and a heart as big as the Appalachians. He's a real character—one of a kind." Cassie was excited at the prospect of seeing Pop again.

It seemed to Cassie only a short time since they had taken off in Tony's private jet, and now they were experiencing their final descent into the Louisville airport.

It had been a beautiful, but uneventful, flight, as Cassie had found herself viewing her imminent reunion with mixed emotions. *Would Pop like Tony?* Cassie pondered, afraid that she already knew the answer. He wasn't David, but maybe Pop would accept Tony just because she was going to marry him. *Oh please, Pop,* she silently pleaded, *like him. It will make everything so much easier.*

As the tires of the Saikas jet hit the runway and bounced, Cassie's contemplation came to an end.

"We're here, darling," Tony said as he reached for her hand and looked out the window. "We'll be unloading shortly, and then in a little less than two hours we'll be at the famous Delaney Farms, deep in the Appalachian heartland," he quipped lightly.

Cassie cast him a side glance as his jovial mood continued. "Do I have to ask Pop's permission for your hand in marriage...or do I just offer a few horses and a couple of cows for the price of the bride?"

Cassie laughed at his verbal antics. "Pop has enough animals to look after. His price would probably be fifty pounds of chocolate, several baseball caps, and...yes, a new truck. 'Tinker' is over thirty years old and as Pop says, 'she's a gettin' right ornery.'"

"Tinker?" Tony asked quizzically. "I know I shouldn't ask, but why Tinker?"

"Because Pop says all he ever does is tinker with her. He goes on about her a lot, but, for all her problems, she's like an old friend to him."

"You're right, Pop does sound like a character...and darling, I really do want him to like me. For some reason I feel as if Pop is the key to your giving me a definite yes. If I win Pop over then I win you. Right?" he asked pointedly.

"I don't know, Tony...we'll see," Cassie hedged as she tried to forget her silent plea to Pop. "But I do need to warn you—Pop can be pretty direct about some things; and, if I know Pop, he'll try to arrange some time to be alone with you for what he calls man-to-man jawing! So be prepared!"

"No problem. I'll be very cooperative," he said, continuing to hold her hand as they disembarked from his jet.

A rented car awaited them at the edge of the field, and soon they were on their way to Delaney Farms. As the mountains came into view, Cassie felt a thrill of expectancy and a restless energy engulfed her.

"It won't be long, Tony, only a few more miles.

There, turn onto that small paved road. Take the next right onto a dirt road and the first graveled drive you come to will be home—Delaney Farms."

Tony did as instructed and Cassie could not contain her smile as first the barn came into view and finally the Victorian house itself.

"This is it. What do you think?" Cassie asked as she surveyed the familiar scene with pride. "Nothing's changed; it looks just the same."

For a moment Tony examined his surroundings, as if grasping for the right words. "It's quaint, serene, the perfect place to write...I can see why you came here."

"Oh, Tony, I'm glad you like it. Let's get out and find Pop. I hope he's home. Usually he mucks stalls..." Cassie did not finish her sentence before the barn door opened, and Pop Bailey appeared. Seeing the strange car, he walked steadily toward the uninvited visitors. Cassie waved, but Pop did not respond; he only walked a little faster toward the couple.

"Pop," Cassie finally called as she ran to meet him, "Don't you recognize me? It's Cassie."

"Cassie, lil' Cassie...Well, I'll be. I didn't recognize ya with all them city clothes on and that new hairdo," he said as he reached out and hugged her. "Why didn't ya let me know ya was comin? I'd a had things ready for ya!" He looked past Cassie to Tony, who was still standing by the car.

Cassie looked at Tony but did not respond to the unasked question which she saw in Pop's eyes. "I...we...thought we'd surprise you...," Cassie stammered awkwardly.

Pop looked at her steadily as he bluntly asked, "Who's we?"

Cassie forced a smile and nodded in Tony's direction. "That, Pop, is Tony Saikas, my boss. Come on, I want you two to meet." Putting her arm through the old man's, she started to walk in Tony's direction.

Pop didn't move. Instead, he nodded his head

slightly at Tony and looked back at Cassie. "And…?"

"And," Cassie replied weakly, "he's asked me to marry him."

"That so," observed Pop as he finally responded to Cassie's leading and walked toward the car.

When he reached the car, Pop extended his hand in greeting and proclaimed, "Mr. Saikus, I'm Pop Bailey. I been told yore Cassie's boss and yore hankering to marry her. Is that right?"

At first the old man's directness and penetrating gaze shook Tony's composure, but he quickly recovered and, shaking Pop's calloused hand firmly, he smoothly responded, "Yes, Mr. Bailey, I am Cassandra's employer, I do want to marry her, and I'd like your permission."

Pop eyed him thoughtfully. Then, as he stooped to unload the car, he said, "Ya would? Well, that'll take some time and a good bit of jawing. First things first. Let's unload the car and get ya settled."

"Cassie, in my travels, I don't think I've ever spent the night in a Victorian farmhouse…I…" Tony's sentence was left hanging as Aubry interrupted.

"Don't mean to be unfriendly, Mr. Saikus, seeing how yore a guest and all…but it ain't proper for yew and Cassie to spend the night in the same house together…alone. I know things are different in the big city, but this ain't the big city. Yew can bunk with me," he said as he reached for Tony's luggage. "Here, I'll take yurs to my place. Yew take Cassie's up to the main house, and I'll be up directly." Without looking in Tony's direction, Pop picked up the luggage and headed for the brick path that wound past the house to the log cabin.

Tony stood there with disbelief written on his face. His mouth flew to protest, but he kept silent when he felt Cassie touch his arm and saw her shake her head gently. When Pop was out of earshot, he looked at Cassie and said, with an edge of harshness in his voice, "I don't believe him! Who does he think he is? This isn't the eighteenth century and you're over twenty-one…and besides," he added, "he shouldn't worry—you can wear a white wedding dress."

"Tony, Pop looks at things differently. He loves me, I'm all he has, and this is his way of protecting me, that's all. It's nothing personal. He's just old-fashioned. Please try to understand. Please, for me?"

A brief look of frustration flashed in Tony's dark eyes as he struggled to respond with understanding. "Okay, I'll try. He may be just trying to protect you…but I'm not so sure it isn't personal." Tony picked up her bags, and they walked toward the house.

Cassie opened the front door and eagerly walked into the living room. For a moment, she forgot that Tony was standing behind her as her eyes surveyed the familiar things she loved—the couch facing the large window, the worn rug, the checker game, the fireplace, her grandparents' antiques. Everywhere she looked she saw memories—memories of David.

"Where do you want me to put your things?" Tony inquired from behind.

"In my room, at the top of the stairs, first door on the left. I'll open the windows while you're doing that and let in some fresh air." She added to herself, "And maybe let *out* some painful *memories.*"

Chapter Fourteen

Cassie was plumping up some down cushions when she heard Pop's familiar whistling approach the house. "Come on in, Pop, I'm in here," Cassie called through the open window of the living room.

Tony was descending the stairs just as Pop entered the house and tried to make light conversation with the old man. "You've got a nice place here, Mr. Bailey. You must know a great deal about farming after running Delaney Farms for all these years. Cassandra's told me you're the backbone of this place," Tony concluded with an uneasy grin.

"Yup, I been here a long time, and if I be knowing anythang, I learnt it from Cassie's Grandpa," Pop said matter-of-factly as he sat down on the hearth and studied the checker board, still set up for a game that never was played.

"Mr. Saikus, yew play checkers?" Pop asked dryly.

"Not since I was a kid. I really prefer chess, but it's been years since I've played even that," Tony replied. He motioned for Cassie to join him on the couch.

"Well, that's a shame. Cassie's Grandpa always use to say ya really get to know a body when ya play him a game of checkers....sittin' across from him, eyeball to eyeball, ya might say. Yep, shore get to know a body." He gestured toward Cassie. "Now lil' Cassie there, she likes to play chess, too. She played a lot while she was here writin' her book."

"How many times did she beat you?" Tony asked jokingly.

"Oh, *I* don't play no chess. Too confusing...with all them knights and kings and popes and whoever else is on the board. Nope, I like checkers," Pop replied.

Cassie quickly broke in, "Pop, how's Nadia doing? I've really missed her."

"Oh, she's doing fine. Beginning to show good, and, if she keeps growing the way she is, I figure we gonna have us a mighty fine filly by April," Pop declared proudly.

"A filly? Pop, how can you be so sure it's going to be a filly?"

"If we're gonna build a nice herd of horses, we'll be needin' a filly...and our needs ain't never been ignored yet," Pop said matter-of-factly as he got up from the hearth and stretched his legs. "Tell ya what girl, why don't ya finish my chores? I was fixing to give Nadia her rubdown and clean her hooves when yew two showed up. Why don't ya go visit with her for a spell, and me and Mr. Saikus will take Tinker into town. I need to get some feed and a few things for yur cupboards." Pop glanced at Tony, still sitting on the couch.

"Mr. Bailey," Tony hedged, "maybe I could be of more use here."

"Nope," Pop broke in easily, "Figured, since ya don't play checkers, we can get some of our jawing done on the way to town," Pop finished, as he eyed Tony intently.

Tony stood up and amiably replied, "Well, since you put it that way, let's go...but we can take my car."

"I appreciate the offer...but I just wouldn't feel right leaving old Tinker behind. 'Sides, I got a lot of feed to pick up and that little car ain't hardly big enough to hold it all." Gesturing at Tony's clothes, Pop added, "And if ya brung some duds that ain't quite so fancy, ya best be puttin' 'em on. Tinker ain't the cleanest truck yul ever see."

Tony eyed his suede blazer and nodded in agreement with the old caretaker. "Perhaps you're right. Where do I go?"

"Just go out the front door and hit that brick path to yur left, go straight toward that thicket, and my log cabin is right there. Go on in, door's unlocked...I'll meet ya on the front porch directly," Pop instructed.

Tony turned to Cassie. "Well, darling, it looks as if you're going to be by yourself for a while. Think you can stay out of trouble while I'm gone?"

"I'll be too busy taking care of Nadia to get into trouble." Cassie countered lightly. Tony slipped his arm around her shoulders as they walked toward the door.

Cassie saw Pop's stern glance at Tony's arm resting possessively on her shoulders, and it made her feel uneasy. She turned casually and walked toward the library table behind the couch, freeing herself from Tony's nearness.

"Oh, Pop, I almost forgot," she said as she reached for her purse on the table. "Something for you," she said as she opened her purse and produced a thick bar of chocolate. "There's a shop in New York called the Sweet Shop and it has candies from all over the world. Knowing your love for chocolate, I couldn't resist. This one is from Switzerland."

"Now girl, what am I gonna do with ya? Mmmmm...my mouth's watering."

Tony stood at the edge of the room and watched the gentle interaction between the old man and the young woman, and scowled faintly at their obvious closeness. "Cassandra," Tony interrupted the brief exchange, "I think I'll go and change. See you in a few minutes."

Cassie turned and answered warmly, "I need to change, too. I'll try to get back down before you two leave. If not, I'll meet you at the barn when you return. Maybe we can go for a hike or a ride before dark. I want to show you all of Delaney Farms."

"Sounds good," Tony said as he reluctantly turned to go.

Cassie watched Pop's crusty hands fiddle with the ornate wrapping paper. "They mean fer ya to eat this stuff, or is it just suppose to be purty to look at?" Pop sputtered in mild exasperation.

"Oh, give me that," Cassie jokingly ordered as she took the candy and deftly unwrapped it.

At first Pop took only a small bite. As the smooth taste filled his mouth, he grinned like a child with a brand new toy.

"Shore do like ya bringing this to me. Wish I could say the same thing 'bout that city feller," Pop stated flatly as his twinkling blue eyes lingered on Cassie's face.

"Pop, you're not being fair! You haven't even given him a chance. You don't even know him," Cassie argued defensively.

"Well, yur right 'bout that. This is the first time I ever saw him. He's right friendly, got polite ways, and talks nice enough. Yep, I can see how a body could like him, but, honey, there's something 'bout him that don't seem quite right—like he ain't what he's tryin to be," Pop concluded gently as he took another bite of the delicious candy.

Cassie walked irritably away from Pop and absently straightened a picture before she spoke her next words. "Pop, I didn't think you'd like him," Cassie said softly as she turned to face him, "and I don't want to hurt you, but Tony has asked me to marry him, and I intend to say yes," she added firmly.

Pop's wise old eyes looked at her sadly as he saw the hardened countenance that had replaced her familiar sweet expression. "Girl, I told ya 'fore, I can't tell ya what to do. But if yur mind was done made up and if ya knowd I weren't goin' to care for him, why'd ya even bother to bring him here?" questioned Pop.

"Since you're the only family I have, I just...I just

wanted the two of you to meet, that's all," Cassie answered lamely.

"It won't wash, girl. All the figures just don't add up. Ya came back from that big city sayin' yew was writin' a book, but there was more to it than that, though I never askt. Then ya lived here and met Doc Dave and said that ya loved him, but ya wanted yur work, too; so ya ran back to New York. Now yur back here with this here Tony sayin yur fixin' to get married. When did ya stop lovin' David McBride and start lovin' this here Saikus fella?" questioned the wise old man.

A lump rose in Cassie's throat. Vainly she struggled for the right answer as his caring eyes watched her reaction.

"Cassie," Pop gently asked, "Do you love Tony Saikus? Have ya forgotten the Doc so soon?"

Cassie flushed. She had never lied to Pop before and she couldn't now. "Pop," she began with all the strength she could muster, "You once told me that love wasn't always enough...well, just maybe it's not always *necessary*. And David," she continued sharply, "is evidently far different from what I thought."

Without giving Pop a chance to speak, she walked toward the staircase and spoke to him over her shoulder. "If I'm going to brush Nadia I'd better change. Tell Tony I'll see him in the barn after you get back." Saying that, she hurried up the stairs.

Pop felt the crinkly texture of the wrapper as he removed the last piece of candy. He stood still, gazing at the now-empty staircase. A tear glistened on the weathered old cheek as he felt Cassie's anger and frustration blanket him like a dense fog.

"Oh, girl," Pop whispered in the muted room, "What's happened to ya? What foolishness are ya fixin' to do? Marryin' a man ya don't love. Tryin' to forgit one ya do. What's it goin' to take? I wonder...."

Slowly his old face brightened as he peered up the stairs, then out the window to see if Tony were approaching. He stood still and held his breath while listening for any noise that would interrupt his plan.

Quickly and carefully, Pop walked to the telephone. His right hand reached for the receiver, and he eased his left finger under it and held down the button. Not until the receiver was securely against his ear did he release the button and let the dial tone blare.

Cautiously, he dialed the familiar number. As each digit was completed, he prayed that the phone would be answered quickly. Finally, after the third ring, came the voice he had been so anxious to hear.

"Doc Dave, this here's Pop," whispered the caretaker. "I can't talk long and I shore can't talk loud, but ya need to know Cassie's back—and she brung that city feller with her. She's goin' to the barn shortly and I'm takin Fancy Pants to town. No time to listen to yur words—I think I here someone comin'!" Pop quickly hung up the phone and walked toward the front door.

He stopped short of the door when he realized that the only thing he had heard had been the rapid beat of his own heart. "I ain't never been one to sneak 'round or speak slyly," he muttered softly. "Good thing too. I'd be plum dead by now," he said, as he placed his hand over his chest and took several deep breaths.

Placing his hand on the door knob, he looked back up the stairs and spoke to an absent Cassie. "Girl, I can't tell ya which gent to choose…but I can try an' see that ya get a choice."

By the time Pop reached the sidewalk, his heartbeat had returned to normal, and his breathing was easier. "Them's the clothes ya brung to wear on a farm?" he asked, as Tony crossed over from the brick path to meet him. "Ain't ya never been on no farm?" Aubry questioned as he eyed Tony's khaki slacks, blue madras shirt, and leather belt, with its expensive gold buckle.

"Mr. Bailey, my parents own a place in the country not far from Saratoga…about three hundred acres. We run about eighty horses, so you might say I'm familiar with the country," Tony replied sarcastically.

"Suit yerself, but I bet ya ain't got nothin like Tinker on yur place," Pop said as he headed toward the battered blue truck, parked adjacent to the barn.

"Where's Cassie?" Tony questioned.

"Oh, she ain't ready yet…said she'd meet ya when we get back. We'd best be going—won't be long 'fore the store'll close. Pete likes to go home kinda early on Saturdays. He'll probably lock up 'round four."

Tony hesitated briefly before joining the older man. Finally, shaking his head somewhat irritably, he shrugged his shoulders and caught up with Pop.

"Mr. Saikus, yur going to have to get in through my side. Tinker's door is jammed, and I just ain't been able to fix it yet. Just move some of that stuff onto the floor and slide across the seat. Careful not to tear yur breeches on that little spring that's poking through. Might help if ya put that livestock catalog under you…could ease the pinch."

Tony smiled thinly at the old man's instructions. His amiable facade of the last few hours was deteriorating with each word that Pop Bailey spoke. "I'll be fine, Mr. Bailey," Tony retorted mildly. "Let's just go, so we can get this over with and I can get back to Cassandra. So far we've had very little time together…alone," he added while maneuvering to avoid the spring that twisted in the center of the passenger's seat.

"Well, Mr. Saikus," Pop said easily as the ancient truck made several false starts before lurching onto the gravel drive, "yur in for a real treat. Some folks say Tinker's a real antique. Bet ya know lot about antique cars," Pop ventured, as they continued to jostle along, even after turning onto the paved road.

Tony gritted his teeth as he forced a friendly response. "I know a little bit about antique cars. I've bought and sold a few, but even though, ah, Tinker's a fine truck, I don't think she's old enough to be classified as an antique—not yet anyway."

Pop shot Tony a side glance, hoping to see the expression on his face, especially in his eyes. Pop knew that a voice could fool you, but a body's eyes showed what was in a man's heart.

The old truck continued its rough trip toward town at its top speed, thirty-five miles per hour. Pop usually enjoyed the ride, but usually he rode alone or shared the cab with a friend. Today was different.

"Mr. Saikus," Pop began deliberately. "Why don't we cut the sweet talk, and get to what's on both our minds—Cassie. Yur hankerin' to marry her and somethin' tells me that yur thinkin' if ya get me on yur side then you'll get Cassie. That sound about right?"

"You're very astute, Mr. Bailey. I want your permission, because I want Cassie and, if it takes winning you over, that's what I'll do," Tony admitted levelly.

"Feared it ain't that simple," came Pop's brief reply. "From where I sit I don't think yur the one for Cassie. You've been sayin ya want Cassie, but I ain't heard ya mention once ya love her."

"It's the same thing," was Tony's strained reply, as he sought to shift his weight off the broken spring.

"When ya *want* somebody, it's cause yur thinking what's best for *yew*…but when ya *love* a body, then yur wantin' what's best for *them.* Which is it—love or want?" Pop asked again.

Tony's nerves were fraying more and more from the slow monotonous ride, the jab of the spring with each bounce of the seat, and Pop's persistent examination. "Okay, *love!* I love her. Does that satisfy you?" he exclaimed.

"Maybe, maybe not. How's yur magazine doin? Cassie said there was some big problems and that's why she returned to New York in such a hurry."

"Everything's fine, Mr. Bailey, just fine. Couldn't be better. In fact…" Tony's words were left hanging as Pop broke in thoughtfully.

"Yep, real interesting. Cassie told me 'bout working

169

so hard these last few years to make that magazine a big success. Then there's a big problem and she goes back and things are smooth again. Guess it's just a coincidence," Pop calmly observed as he felt, more than saw, Tony's glare.

"Cassandra and I are a team, and we do things together, and we make things happen together. That magazine and her career mean everything to Cassandra."

"Seems ya got a lot to larn 'bout that girl. Ya don't really know her at all," Pop said dryly.

"I know enough about Cassandra to know that with me she can be both very successful and famous—if you don't rock the boat," Tony added heatedly. "I plan to marry Cassandra, whether you like it or not!"

Pop's truck came to a halt as it approached the town's one and only stop sign. He looked at Tony Saikas and felt himself shiver as he saw the unvarnished contempt in those cold, dark eyes.

At last Pop saw into the soul of Tony Saikas, and knew that this man's plans for his lil' Cassie would lead to no good.

The familiar smell of leather and wood shavings greeted Cassie as she lifted the wooden latch and opened the heavy barn door. The sights and smells excited pleasant memories of her childhood years spent tending the chores with her grandad and Pop.

As she walked into the coolness of the dark barn, Cassie relished the tranquility of the moment. A low whinny told her that Nadia had heard her and waited expectantly. Cassie went into the tack room and picked up a bridle of soft, dark leather, and smiled when she noticed the suppleness of it. Obviously Pop had been cleaning and oiling it regularly.

She took a brush from the shelf and made her way to the stall where Nadia stood, her beautiful head thrust forward over the gate. "How you doing, little mama?"

170

Cassie crooned, remembering the foal that was due in April.

Cassie rubbed the shapely head, admiring the wide-set eyes and the velvety white blaze that extended down to flaring nostrils. Nadia's dark coat was sleek and shiny.

"I can see Pop's been feeding you well. You're fat and sassy," she said, opening the stall door and slipping a bridle over the mare's head.

Tying her up, Cassie left the stall door open and began to brush her. "You're still muscular as ever. Pop must be turning you out to run. That's what *I'd* like to do, girl—run."

The vocal confession startled Cassie and she laughed as she thought, *Did I mean run Nadia or run away?*

The crucial decisions and pressures of the last few months evaporated as Cassie lost herself in the pleasant, simple task of caring for her horse. The security of her childhood seemed to recapture her, and it was as if she were a child again.

She pushed aside the uneasy decision to marry Tony; she forgot the pressures of her job. All of the surface turmoils seemed to vanish for a brief moment of escape. Then the deep longing and emptiness which she had buried under a frenzy of work and activity forced their way into her mind.

She had refused to acknowledge them since the night that Tony had asked her to marry him. She had made her decision, and David McBride was no longer any part of her life. She drew a sharp, quick breath, as pain from deep within her subconscious surfaced, and she felt anew the anguish of a life without David.

The brush stopped in mid-air as she leaned against the horse, overcome for a moment. Then she slowly shook her head and resumed her brushing.

A noise directly behind her jarred her into the present. When she turned, her eyes widened and she dropped the brush as she saw David McBride leaning against the adjacent post staring at her steadily!

"Dav—David?" she asked, almost in a whisper. "What are you doing here?"

"Watching you," was his quiet response.

"I mean here, in Kentucky," Cassie stammered.

"I live here."

"I thought you went back to St. Louis."

"I did, but not to stay."

"David, I don't understand," she said, finally overcoming the shock.

"What is it you don't understand?" His blue eyes held hers in their warm, magnetic grip.

"You know—St. Louis, Priscilla, New York."

"Didn't you know my father was ill?" he inquired with surprise.

"Yes, I knew that, but Priscilla said you had accepted your dad's offer."

"Oh, Priscilla? So that's it," he said, his surprise fading. "I did accept his offer— his offer to support a hospital here."

"What?" she asked weakly.

"You know how I feel about this place," was his calm reply.

"But what about New York? And Priscilla?"

"I was in New York to close the sale on Dad's clinics. Priscilla is his attorney, and that's why she was there. It took two days to take care of all the details," he patiently explained to her as he would to a small child. Then, with a smile, he added, "And do I need to add—we stayed in separate rooms?"

"You're not going to stay in St. Louis and marry Priscilla?"

"Cassie." He spoke her name softly, with the tenderness of a caress. "Cassie, there's only one woman I love, and I told her I'd be here waiting. I love you. These months have seemed like an eternity without you."

"Why didn't you call or write?" she asked, her dark eyes bright with unshed tears.

David reached his hand out as if to pull her to him but then dropped it to his side and said, "Darling, the only way it'll work for us is if you come back to me because you want to and because you know that it's the right thing to do. I won't force you. It has to be your own decision."

A heavy silence hung between them as David searched Cassie's face for an answer. Then, when he could find none, he asked, "Cassie, have you come back to me?"

She dropped her eyes from his before she could answer. "No, David, I'm going to marry Tony Saikas."

"Why?" The word exploded from him so forcefully that Cassie flinched.

"That will be best for all of us," she answered evasively, refusing to meet his eyes.

"Do you love him?"

"My mind is made up. It's settled," she said, turning her back on him before he could see the pain and longing in her eyes.

Just as she picked up the brush once again, David grabbed her shoulder and spun her around. Putting his large hands on both shoulders, he pressed her against the stall, demanding, "Look at me, Cassandra Delaney, and tell me you love him and not me!"

Still she refused to look at him, so he released one shoulder and lifted her head with his hand until she *had* to meet his eyes. But she would not answer.

They stood like that for several seconds—David waiting for the answer to ease his hurt; Cassie seeing the pain she had inflicted but unable to do anything about it.

"I know the answer," he finally said as he dropped his hands from her. His face was a study of anguish and disgust. "You don't love him. It's your ambition. If it were Tony, I would fight for you because I know you don't love him. But I can't fight your stubborn will, and that's the real tragedy. You think you want success, in order to

173

have fulfillment, but you won't find that until you look beyond yourself for direction for your life."

David stood watching her in silence. His hands were by his sides and anger had replaced the tenderness in his eyes. He watched the color drain from her face. Then, without another word, he turned and walked out of the barn.

She did not move or speak. From somewhere down the lane she heard the faint sound of his landrover as it cranked up and drove away.

The unshed tears refused to come and offer their relief. She felt as if she had died inside. It took a few minutes for any feeling to return. When it did, she had an overwhelming urge to escape—from Tony, from David, from his accusations, from the hurt look in his eyes, and mostly from *herself*.

Impulsively, Cassie untied Nadia, mounted the mare's bare back, and rode out of the barn.

Chapter Fifteen

David's parting words haunted Cassie as she began to canter down the broad trail where they had raced in early spring. The memory of that earlier ride was etched in her mind like delicate flowers on fine crystal.

With his admonition ringing in her ears, she admitted to herself that nothing in New York could equal the joy that she had experienced on that evening and on others spent with him. It seemed strange to Cassie that her phenomenal success since returning to her career had not diminished the joys they had shared or eased the longing for him. How could the sharing of dreams with someone surpass the realization of them?

Yet she remembered her moment of truth after seeing David in New York, when she had admitted that her decision to leave him had been wrong. Why, then, in the barn, had she still refused to admit her love to him?

Cassie tried in vain to dismiss the painful questions as she opened Nadia to a full gallop. The trail forked to the left, and horse and rider continued on with increasing speed. Only Cassie's state of mind allowed her to let the powerful mare have her head on an unfamiliar trail. Cassie had been cautioned when she had bought Nadia that racehorse blood flowed in her veins. Cassie had respected that information and kept the Arabian mare under tight control...until now.

The horse felt her mistress relax the reins and surged forth with a new burst of power. Like the wind they whisked through the forest. The pounding hooves matched the pounding of Cassie's heart and the trees passed by like blankets of green.

The broad trail began to narrow, and its smoothness was interrupted by boulders here and there, as the level plain started upward. Cassie fought to bring the horse under control, Pop's warning ringing in her head.

"One thing ya allus have to remember, Cassie girl. Ya gotta let the horse know who's in control. Horses are just like people—if they get their head then they'll sure run theirselves to destruction and yew with 'em! But if all that power is under control, then they can go a lot further and get where they was suppose to be safely."

Oh, Pop, is that what's wrong with me, wanting to control my own life? That's what David said, and he said I'd never be happy. Is that where I'm going to end, destroying myself and the ones who love me? she thought as she continued to pull on the reins.

Suddenly Cassie looked ahead and saw a deep crevice. Apparently the erosion of many years had divided the trail with a gully that had widened and deepened with each passing season. Cassie realized too late that she would be unable to turn the mare, so she pressed her knees into the horse's side and prepared for the jump! Only a miracle would take them over the chasm!

She felt the puissant muscles tense and the front feet leave the ground as a great surge of power lifted horse and rider up and into the air. Cassie grabbed Nadia's mane as the wind stung her face and she prepared for the worst.

The horse's front hooves hit the ground, jarring them severely, but miraculously clearing the ravine. It was difficult to maintain her seat. Never had her expert horsemanship proved more valuable. She pulled back on the reins and this time Nadia responded.

They slowed to a gallop and then to a canter as they came out of the woods onto a narrow rocky trail. They had not been more than five hundred yards when Cassie noticed a trail emerging from a dense, evergreen forest and joining her present path. The trail looked familiar; she recognized it as the one she and David had taken on their picnic. She remembered David's telling her that the Wacomaw trail near her house led north to the falls, and she must have found it now.

Cassie and Nadia pulled to a stop and sat in a moment of indecision. Cassie had always promised Pop that she would not ride far away from the house alone, and then only on familiar trails. She had broken every safety rule today! She had ridden bareback, taken a strange trail, and given Nadia her head. She knew better than to go on, but, when she recognized the spot, she felt a strong desire to continue. Heedless of her inner warnings, she moved forward.

They continued to climb upward on the narrow steep path. She kept the reins tight and pressed her knees into Nadia's shoulders as she struggled to keep her seat. The edge of the trail was a sheer drop to the valley below. With an urgency that mystified her, Cassie pushed the tired horse upward. Something within her was drawing her to the place where David had first declared his love. It seemed as if the answers for which she searched would be there.

The urgency pushed aside her normal concern for her mare—and, in her preoccupation, she failed to register the storm clouds gathering southwest of the mountain.

As they rounded a sharp curve, Cassie recognized the last steep grade before the falls. It was then that she noticed the threatening weather. The mid-afternoon light had turned an ominous gray, and she looked up at a large, black cloud.

Realization of her predicament hit her just as the first drops of rain did. She urged Nadia up the last few feet of the treacherous trail to level ground.

Dense clouds covered the spectacular view, and she knew that, within a few moments, they would be deluged, making a return back down the steep trail impossible. She had circled the pool and was nearly at the entrance to the cave when a sharp bolt of lightning, followed by a loud clap of thunder, pierced the air and the torrential downpour began. Suddenly, in one final spurt of energy, Nadia reared, and Cassie slid off the wet horse and onto the boulder-strewn ground!

She lay on the ground, a small, crumpled mass. The mare gingerly picked her way around Cassie and stood looking down, as if in apology. Then, turning, she walked over to the edge of the trail where it began its downward journey and stood patiently waiting. When her mistress didn't retrieve her, Nadia started down the steep trail alone.

Pop and Tony drove up in the yard just before dark. The trip into town had taken longer than expected. Tinker was acting up and the ride home had been interminable.

The old man felt an uneasy disappointment when he saw neither Cassie nor David's rover. He knew the doctor had been there, from the fresh mud-grip treads along the lane. Then disappointment changed to hope as he thought perhaps they had left together to have a talk. "Tony, if you'll grab a couple of sacks, we'll stock up Cassie's larder. Be kind of poor eatin' around here if we hadn't gone in to town," Pop drawled.

The two men got out, unloaded the truck and went into the house. Pop was a little surprised that Cassie had not returned from the barn before she had left with David. He was turning that over in his mind when he heard Tony say, "Mr. Bailey, are you all right?"

"What? What's that you say?"

"I asked if you knew where Cassie is."

"Oh, she's probably out there with them horses. Can't get enough of 'em. I just don't see how she can ever be happy up there in that big city away from all this."

"No problem. I'll just buy a place big enough for the horses, and you can move there and take care of them," Tony answered lightly.

"Whoa, there! I ain't leavin' these hills. I came here over fifty years ago, and I plan to die here. Somebody's gotta see to the ole home place."

"I doubt seriously if Cassandra will want to keep it when we're married. I think it'd be best if she cut her ties with this place. You know, painful memories and all," Tony answered smoothly. "I'll go see if she's in the barn."

"Why don't ya just freshen up a bit and rest a spell after yur long day. The bathroom's down the hall. I'll go fetch Cassie since I got to finish up the feedin' anyhows."

"I'm not tired, but I do need to make a phone call or two. Just tell her I'm waiting," Tony responded as he turned to leave the room.

Pop went out the back door and across the porch, his old face lined with concern. The more he thought about it, the more he knew Cassie wouldn't have gone off with David without leaving him word, especially with Tony here. He could see the barn door standing ajar, and that disturbed him even more. He had taught her never to leave it open, and all her life she had been careful to follow his rules. No, something must be wrong—he could feel it in his bones.

As he approached the barn, Aubry could see that Nadia's stall was empty. Then he knew that Cassie had gone for a ride. It eased his worry some, but it still wasn't like her to go off without a note or to leave the door open. *Oh well, maybe it blew open,* he thought as he went into the feed room. *Things shore must not have went good at all. Maybe the ride'll clear her thinking. I shore hope something does afore she marries that dandy up yonder.*

Pop took a bucket and filled it with feed for Shebazzi, who was whinnying for his dinner. He went through the stall, rubbing a caressing hand down the proud stallion's back, and opened the opposite gate that led to the paddock. "Come on, fella. Let these tired old eyes see ya prance."

Shebazzi pleased Pop; the stallion had sired some fine young ones. In a couple of years Delaney Farms might be known once again for its fine horseflesh. "That is, if Fancy Pants don't have his way and sell the place," Pop muttered under his breath.

Pop pushed the thought from his mind as he marveled at the sinewy majesty of the proud stallion. The old caretaker climbed up on the board fence to sit down and enjoy the show. He heard a low rumble. The heavily forested hills hampered his view of the gathering storm, but he could tell by the behavior of the high-strung animal that bad weather was on its way.

He whistled for the horse and rattled the feed bucket. Shebazzi's prancing turned into a lope as he made his way back to the stall and his feed.

Just as Pop was filling the last waterbucket, Tony walked into the barn. "Where's Cassandra? I thought you said she'd be in the barn—?"

"Yup, I should'a knowed better'n that. She's out riding her mare," he explained amiably.

"I wish she had waited; I could have joined her."

"Couldn't have. We ain't got nothin' else for ya to ride," Pop explained.

"What about that horse? He's a really fine-looking animal."

"No siree, couldn't let ya ride him; ya see, only *real experienced* riders can handle him."

"Well, I'm experienced," Tony stated firmly.

"No, ya don't understand, I mean *expert* riders. No, I just couldn't chance it. The horse might get spooked and break a leg or something and he's worth a lot of money to Delaney Farms."

Tony said nothing else. He just looked at the old man. His lips had a slight smile on them, but his eyes were cold and calculating. "It gets dark early here, doesn't it?" he asked, changing the subject.

"No, the good Lord gives us the same amount of daylight as anybody else. We just got a storm brewing. Guess we'd better go to the house."

"What about Cassandra? Shouldn't she be back?"

"No worry 'bout Cassie. She don't ever go fer by herself and she'll come back afore it rains," Pop commented, with more confidence than he felt. "I'll be with ya in just a minute; let me put up this bucket." Pop turned to go through the tack room, and his heart sank when he glanced at the saddle rack. Nadia's saddle was still in its place! Now he knew for certain that there was trouble brewing. He realized that Cassie would not have left it behind if she hadn't been upset or in a hurry.

The creases in his old face deepened as he shook his head sadly and thought, *Maybe I shouldn't have called Doc. I never interfered in Cassie's life before. I gave her advice only when she asked for it. Yeh, guess I did put in a good word for the Doc once or twice right at the beginnin'; but I kept my hands off and my mouth closed after she went back to New York.*

In his wisdom he had realized that this had been one situation that the "Good Lord would have to handle," and Cassie would have to make her own choices.

Pop could have told her that God's way was the only way she'd ever be happy, but *the Good Lord never forced Hisself on anyone, and I guess 'til she believes it for herself, my believin' it won't do no good. Yessir, when it comes to the Lord a body has to believe it for theirselves. It shore hurts me to think of that little tyke having such a sad lonely time at school that it turned her all bitter where she just couldn' believe God cared anything about her anymore or was interested in her being happy. Course, I seen it afore. A person's got two choices when heartaches come, they can turn and blame God or they can scrooch up closer and get some comfort. Like the Good Book says, the rain falls on them that's just and them that's unjust. Life's that way.*

He sighed before saying aloud, "Yep, shore hope callin' David wasn't steppin in the Lord's affairs."

"Did you say something, Bailey?" Tony asked curtly from just outside the barn.

"I'm just thinking out loud, and I'm thinking we ought to hav a cup o' coffee and some sweet rolls Doc Dave's housekeeper sent over. Would you like some?"

"Very well. Who is Doc Dave?"

"Dr. David McBride, our doctor here in the valley and up in the hills. Lives on the place next to ours."

At the mention of David McBride's name, a dark scowl crossed Tony's handsome, finely chiseled features. "Oh, yes, I met him once in New York. I thought he moved to St. Louis."

"Say you met him? How'd that come about?" he asked unabashedly.

"Cassandra and I went to the theater one night and ran into him with an old friend of mine, Priscilla Bellwood."

"Oh," said Pop, as his understanding deepened. "Say he was in New York at a show with Prissybelle—"

"No, Priscilla Bellwood. Do you know her?" Tony asked, with a puzzled look.

"Yup, met her once. Sure is a purty piece of fluff. I'm not surprised you know her. I'd expect she's yur type."

Tony's irritation with Pop's jibes finally had worn through his cool composure. "What do you mean, 'my type?' "

"Oh she's real purty and a fancy talker and dresser. You know, real 'uptown' like. Now my lil' Cassie, she's more plain folks, if ya be knowing what I mean."

"Bailey," Tony dropped any pretense of civility as he looked directly into Pop's eyes, "you're wrong about Cassandra and," he paused, "she's not anybody's little Cassie."

The coldness in Tony's eyes sent frosty chills down Pop's back.

Once inside, Pop hurriedly prepared the coffee and set out the sweet rolls, hoping that the tasks would somehow take his mind off the weather and Cassie's disappearance. Even so, his eyes kept straying toward the barn, and he lingered longer at the window each time he went by.

Just as a sharp bolt of lightning illuminated the growing darkness outside, the rain began to pour. Gusty winds whistled through the trees, and Pop could conceal his concern no longer.

As he went to the window to watch and wait, the fury of the storm increased. He prayed that Cassie had found shelter somewhere in the woods beyond.

Tony came to stand by him and remarked, "Surely this isn't normal behavior for Cassandra. She shouldn't have gone off like this—and it won't happen again."

Pop ignored Tony's remark with its ominous overtones. "May the Good Lord protect her!" Pop shouted and ran out the door into the driving rain.

From the doorway Tony saw Pop grab the reins of a mud-caked horse and walk with her toward the barn. Tony started out but looked up at the sheets of rain pouring down and returned to stare out the window instead.

Within five minutes, a soaking-wet Pop was back in the room. "That's the mare Cassie rode, and she's got a ugly gash on her leg. I don't know where she's been but Cassie ain't with her. I gotta call Doc and tell him."

"You'll do no such thing. This is my affair, not his, and we'll handle it without his help. Surely the rain will stop soon."

"Great balls of fire, man! Have ya took leave of yur senses? Cassie is probably hurt somewhere up in them woods, *way* up there by the looks of Nadia. She'll need a doctor, and I need someone to find her."

"*Not David McBride*," Tony said.

"The only way ya can stop me is to kill me, and I know even yew ain't that crazy," the old man said quietly as he picked up the phone and dialed the operator.

"Vera? This here's Pop Bailey. Got me a 'mergency; get Doc Dave quick as you can and then call the vet and tell him I need him over here to look at my mare. Yeh, thank ya. No, I'm OK, but I need to talk to the doc."

David answered on the first ring. When he heard the old man's message, he hung up with a terse "I'll be right there."

Tony stood by with a scowl of anger on his face. "Maybe McBride *should* come over here. I want to tell him face to face that Cassandra is no longer any of his concern."

Pop looked at the man in cold silence as he waited for David to arrive. Soon Pop saw the lights of the rover pulling to a stop just outside; and his tall, slicker-coated friend climbed out of the car and ran up the steps.

David opened the door without knocking. "Tell me what happened, Pop," he said as he stepped through the door.

"I don't know. I went in to town like I told you I was goin—"

"What do you mean, old man, *told* him you were? Did you tell him Cassandra was here?" Tony interrupted angrily.

For the first time since entering the room, David looked at Tony. The physician's warm blue eyes turned steel gray as he softly said to Pop, "Go on, Aubry, tell me what happened."

Pop looked from Tony to David and then continued. "When we got back, the barn door was open and Cassie and Nadia was gone. I wasn't so worried at first but then the storm came up, and I found her saddle still in the barn. Then about an hour later, the mare comes back by herself caked in mud with some bad gashes on her. David, what happened 'tween you two this afternoon? Cassie—"

Once again Tony broke in. "Were you here with her while I was gone? How cozy; a lovers' reunion while the fiancé is away. Very convenient."

With one long stride David crossed the space between him and Tony Saikas. His strong arm shot out with bullet speed and grabbed Tony's shirt. David's face was close to the other man's, and the steel gray eyes met the malevolent dark ones. "Let me tell you one thing, Saikas. I don't have time to put up with your insinuations and threats. I'd suggest that you get in your car and leave. If not, just keep out of the way! Do you understand? Cassie's in trouble, and we've got to find her."

With as much dignity as he could muster, Tony said, "Perhaps you're right, McBride. This could be a serious situation, and, since I'm not familiar with the area, I probably could use your help. We'll put our personal differences aside for right now."

Although David stepped back and dropped his hand, he still stared at Tony. With cold determination, he said, "Get one more thing straight, Saikas. You will have *nothing* to do with this search because you'd only hinder our progress. As for our personal differences, you might as well know this—I'll never give Cassie up. If I thought you could make her happy, then I would. But you'll *destroy* her, and I'll never let you do it."

David turned in abrupt dismissal of the speechless Tony and back to Pop. "Do you have any idea where she went?"

Aubry let out a relieved sigh as the crisis eased. "I don't know, David. We allus agreed that when she was alone she wouldn't go far from the house and would stay on the easy, familiar trail, but, from the looks of Nadia, that ain't so this time."

"We'll get the neighbors out and organize a search party. The rain has washed away any tracks, so we'll just have to search the trails one by one. Don't worry, Pop, we'll find her before you know it," David said, with an attempt at a reassuring smile.

David turned toward the telephone to call in help for the long night ahead. He walked by a silent and subdued Tony as if he were not there.

The cold rain pelted Cassie as she lifted her head and slowly looked around. The fall had stunned her, and it took a few seconds for her to get her bearings. Then, remembering, she pushed herself halfway up and weakly called, "Nadia."

The mare was gone! Cassie's heart constricted with fear and her head pounded with pain. Her first thoughts were for the safety of her horse, and she visualized the treacherous trail back down the mountain. Warm tears mixed with cold rain and streamed down her face as she prayed, *Oh, God, protect her—save her from suffering for my foolishness*.

As the events of the afternoon replayed through her mind, she tried to get up. Already the fall was taking its toll, and she felt stiff and sore. She gingerly sat upright and checked her arms, face and pounding head. She then moved her legs, and a sharp pain shot from her left knee to her left ankle. Panic began to mount as she feared a broken leg. Forcibly she dragged herself over to a nearby tree and, with sheer determination, pulled herself up. Then, carefully, she put her weight on her left leg—the pain was excruciating.

A sense of panic churned inside her, clamoring to take control. The wind picked up and bent the small tree she clung to. The cold rain stung her face and she shivered. *Here I am on an isolated mountain, and not one soul knows where I am, and I can't walk. What am I going to do?*

From somewhere out of the panic, she remembered the cave. She looked around and was relieved to see it less than twenty feet from the small tree. She knew that the short trip would be agonizing, but it was her only hope.

Cassie reluctantly dropped back down onto the rain-drenched ground and began her painful crawl.

She was exhausted by the time she had pulled herself

through the rocks and wet mud to the entrance of the cave and had seen the camping supplies which David had stored there for months.

"Thank you, Father," she prayed as she opened up a blanket roll, revealing a lantern and a change of men's clothing. The thought of dry clothing was comforting to the soaked girl, despite her growing anxiety.

Momentarily forgetting the pain in her leg, Cassie tore off her wet shirt that clung like an icy shroud, and put on the flannel one she recognized as David's. Knowing that she could not exchange her jeans for the dry but larger ones, she grabbed the blanket and wrapped it around her. Now that she had alleviated some of her discomfort, she had time to think.

What if no one ever finds me? What if my leg is broken? Is this the way my life will end? She felt the warm tears trickle down her cheeks as she teetered on the brink of panic once more.

Then her reasonable self regained control. "How silly, of course they'll find me. Pop will have someone out looking for me by now so all I'll have to do is wait. But Pop doesn't know about this place—?"

Finally, as the last trace of daylight was swallowed up by darkness, Cassie sat in growing terror and thought about her life and the path which it had taken. All of the doubts that she had pushed aside, all the questions that she had buried, surfaced in the blackness of the cave's night; and the events of her life played before her as on a moving stage. After every heartache had been examined, every struggle conquered, and every success relished, she saw the face of Dr. David McBride, and she remembered the sweet, wondrous joy of his love. Then she acknowledged to herself that, without him, there would be no real life for her.

But Cassie knew that she couldn't share his life until she could share his God. That was the real reason she had rejected David's love; she was afraid of relinquishing control of her own life because she might not get

187

what she wanted. She was afraid that God wouldn't want the same things for her that she did; yet she had obtained everything she had sought, and she still could hear David's haunting question, "But are you happy, Cassie, are you happy?"

Suddenly a cry of anguish broke from Cassie in answer to the question that obsessed her. "No, David, I'm miserable! I want you, and I want your God!"

Then, in the clammy silence that followed her outburst, Cassie began to weep softly as she searched to find the God whom David loved and the One she had turned from so many years before.

"Oh, God," she wept, "help me to know You anew." With those words, Cassie saw into the selfishness of her own soul, and acknowledged her need for Him.

As the sobs racked her small delicate frame, the frustrations of many years washed away. Gone was the anger with a God she thought didn't care; gone were the resentment and bitterness harbored since college days; gone was the fear of failure; and, finally, gone was the determination to rule her own destiny.

When the sobbing subsided, a peaceful and unafraid Cassie, with tired body but renewed spirit, slept deeply the slumber of a newborn infant.

She was oblivious to the frantic searching in the valley below—and she could not see the tired, drawn face of David McBride as he searched on through the rain and wind that filled the night.

The dazzling rays of the early morning sun wakened Cassie just as she heard her name called by a deep and familiar voice.

"David, I'm here, in the cave," she joyously exclaimed as she saw his tall silhouette turn the corner astride Shebazzi.

If Cassie lived to be a hundred years old, she would always cherish the memory of the look on David's face as he rushed into the cave. He hesitated for a split second when he reached the opening. Then, when he saw her, relief flooded every ounce of his being. He ran to her and fell to his knees.

Gathering her into his arms, he crushed her to him as she tried to keep her injured leg out of his way. "Oh, Cassie, Cassie, what did I do to you?" His words spilled out in a flood of concern.

Cassie finally managed to push back from his embrace far enough to see his eyes. "You didn't do anything to me, darling. You were right all the time. Will you still let me share your life?"

She put her hands on either side of his face. The severe stress and fatigue of the night before still held David in their grip. He failed to comprehend what Cassie had said, and replied, "You will never marry Tony Saikas! You belong to me now and forever, do you understand?"

Despite the pain in Cassie's leg, she laughed with sheer joy. "Whatever you say, my love."

David blinked uncomprehendingly. "What did you say, Cassie?"

"I said, whatever you say, my love, now and forever!"

"Do you know what you just said, Cassie?"

"What I've been trying to tell you—I love you!" With that, she pulled his face down to hers and their lips met.

When David released her at last, he asked, "Oh, darling, are you hurt?"

"Yes. My left knee seems to be twisted. I can't put my weight on it. But, David, my heart has been healed!"

As David looked at her radiant countenance, there was no need for any further questions. The renewal was evident in her face. Cassie had finally found her way back home.

Dear Reader:

I am committed to bringing you the kind of romantic novels you want to read. Please fill out the brief questionnaire below so we will know what you like most in Cherish Romances™.

Mail to: Etta Wilson
Thomas Nelson Publishers
P.O. Box 141000
Nashville, Tenn. 37214

1. Why did you buy this Cherish Romance™?

☐ Author
☐ Back cover description
☐ Christian story
☐ Cover art
☐ Recommendation from others
☐ Title
☐ Other_____

2. What did you like best about this book?

☐ Heroine
☐ Hero
☐ Christian elements
☐ Setting
☐ Story Line
☐ Secondary characters

3. Where did you buy this book?

☐ Christian bookstore
☐ Supermarket
☐ Drugstore
☐ General bookstore
☐ Book Club
☐ Other (specify)_____

4. Are you interested in buying other Cherish Romances™?

   ☐Very interested   ☐Somewhat interested
                 ☐Not interested

5. Please indicate your age group.
   ☐Under 18   ☐25-34
   ☐18-24   ☐35-49   ☐Over 50

6. Comments or suggestions?

7. Would you like to receive a free copy of the Cherish Romance™ newsletter? If so, please fill in your name and address.

Name _____

Address _____

City _____ State _____ Zip _____

7361-7